THE CHRISTMAS LODGE

SNOWY PINE RIDGE BOOK ONE

FIONA BAKER

JOIN MY NEWSLETTER

If you love beachy, feel-good women's fiction, sign up to receive my newsletter, where you'll get free books, exclusive bonus content, and info on my new releases and sales!

"Excellent. I'll have my assistant watch for the paperwork and we'll get it signed and returned to you." She listened a few more moments, laughing lightly as he grumbled good-naturedly. "I know, I know, I *do* drive a hard bargain. Have a good night, Paul. Always a pleasure doing business with you."

She dropped the receiver into the cradle with a satisfying *click*, only then allowing herself to jump from her chair and do a victory dance, wiggling her butt and punching the air while whisper-cheering to herself. She was in the middle of a groovy spin when her office door opened softly and her assistant, Brenda, poked her head in.

Lacy stopped mid-spin, her cheeks warming. She cleared her throat, smoothing her hair and straightening her blazer. "Yes, Brenda?"

Brenda was biting back a grin, and Lacy knew it was no use to pretend. She felt her professional facade crack into an infectious grin.

"You saw that, didn't you?" she asked.

Brenda came into the office then, her eyes bright with excitement. "Does that cute little number I just walked in on mean that we got the funding?"

Lacy nodded. "Yes! Paul will be sending over the paperwork for us to sign, either tonight or in the morning, so watch for that."

CHAPTER ONE

"Mr. Cooper, I think we can work out a better deal than that. We've worked together for how many years now? Ten?"

Lacy Preston tucked the phone receiver under her ear as she spoke and swiveled her chair so that she could stare out the window behind her desk, although she quickly realized it was too dark to see anything.

On the other end of the line, Paul Cooper hemmed and hawed for a few more moments before finally conceding, promising to lock in a lower interest rate for the business loan she was currently brokering. The corners of Lacy's lips lifted in pleased smile, but she kept her voice smooth and professional when she responded.

"Will do! That's exciting. I know Cutting Edge Real Estate will be thrilled. This is huge for them."

Cutting Edge, a budding real estate investment company, was one of Lacy's newest clients. They had flipped a handful of homes and made a decent profit, but now they were looking to expand their portfolio by adding rental properties. Taking their business model to the next level meant they needed more financing than she could offer with her own personal investments, which was why the business loan getting approved tonight was such a win.

Lacy dropped back into her leather office chair. "It really is." Glancing at the stylish silver wristwatch she had bought for herself as a graduation present when she graduated with her MBA, she noticed the time. "I didn't realize it was so late. Paul definitely won't be sending the papers tonight. It's almost seven o'clock, Brenda. I'll let you get home."

Brenda congratulated her once more, then slipped back out of Lacy's office, leaving Lacy alone with her thoughts for a moment. She leaned back in her chair, letting out a huge breath and soaking in the moment. Her line of work was often taxing, with its high stress levels and fast pace, but there was nothing like closing a huge deal on a Thursday night to put her in a good mood for Friday and the rest of the weekend. After allowing herself one more moment to exult, Lacy began preparing to go home as well.

She had spent many a late night in this office, poring over financial records for prospective investment deals or hammering out the details of a new business venture, but tonight Lacy decided to go home and open a bottle of wine to celebrate this newest success. As she wound her scarf around her neck and shrugged into a thick peacoat to combat the bitter St. Louis December night, Lacy reflected on her career.

In graduate school, she had created an app for her capstone project that businesses could use to assess their assets, risks, areas for growth, and more. Investors had bought the idea from her, giving her a starting sum to then invest in other businesses. Before she knew it, she had built her own investment and consulting firm, seeking out promising young businesses. She consulted with them and helped watch over their business, as well as giving them an infusion of cash in return for a cut of the profits.

Her line of work was not an easy one, but in her opinion it was well worth it.

The icy wind outside her office whipped against her face, making her catch her breath. She burrowed more deeply into her coat and hurried toward her car.

The only good thing about December in St. Louis is looking forward to Christmas, she thought as she pulled the car door shut behind her, turning the key in the ignition and cranking up the heat.

And it was true. Shops were lit up with twinkling lights, Christmas carols played on all the radio stations, and there was a general air of anticipation and goodwill that made her feel like a child again. Lacy pulled a wry face to herself at that thought.

Of course, it's not like I ever have much time to bask in the holiday spirit, she admitted to herself. *There's always a pile of work waiting for me.*

She didn't mind too much, though. Lacy pulled out of the parking lot and headed toward home, shivering a little on behalf of a man in a Santa suit ringing a bell for donations to charity outside of a shopping center. Shoppers hurried past him, hoping to purchase some gifts before the stores closed for the night, although a few good souls dropped change and dollar bills into his red bucket. The traffic light turned green then, ending her observations, and she continued down the brightly lit streets toward her sleek luxury downtown apartment.

An hour or so later, Lacy settled onto her plush sofa, a glass of white wine in hand. She'd turned soft music on, not wanting to watch TV that night. Taking a sip of her wine, she sank into the cushions, leaning her head back and closing her eyes.

She let the tension ease out of her shoulders and took in a deep breath, savoring the feeling of decadently-soft silk pajamas and that freshly-clean feeling she always loved after her nightly skincare routine. She loved these moments of rest, especially when they came with the satisfaction of a job well done and that her career was moving forward the way she wanted.

Her career was everything to her. Most people she knew had built their careers some time in college or after, but she had been focused on her path since the tender age of eleven years old. Lacy lifted her wine glass, this time taking a long drink. If she was going to think about her past, she needed more than a dainty sip. She closed her eyes again, going back through the years and remembering the night that had changed the trajectory of her life forever.

The night of her eleventh birthday, she had waited to open her presents or have a slice of cake until her father returned from work to celebrate with them. The presents in all their shiny wrapping paper and bright bows had been so tempting, but she had remained steadfast, running to the window every time a car drove by their house in the hopes that it was her father.

Minutes, and then hours, had ticked by with no sign of Harv Spielman. Finally, around bedtime, her mother had come to her, her own eyes red and swollen from crying and her lips tight in an angry line. She had announced that Harv wasn't coming home that night, or ever.

She had been too young to understand at the time why her father had abandoned them, but over the years her mother had explained how her father had turned tail and run away when his investment business had gone south, forcing him to file for bankruptcy. Lacy's mother stopped trying to protect her from the awful truth by the time Lacy finished middle school, telling her about how Harv's business practices were all-too-often shady and deceitful, and how he had never let her in on the details.

"Only a coward would do what he did. Don't you ever forget that," her mother would say on one of the many instances of recounting Harv's past sins. "He didn't run an honest business and, when it all fell apart, what did he do? He abandoned his wife and child, ran back with his tail between his legs to his daddy." At this point in the story, Lacy's mother would always give a bitter laugh. "As if old Nicholas Spielman could help him! His father was part of his business in the first place, which can't say much for his own integrity or business sense. Nicholas turned tail and ran too, just like his son." She'd always tuck Lacy under her chin then, wrapping her arms around her daughter. "We don't need them, though, do we? No, we've got each other, and you'll grow up better without them."

And Lacy had done her best to fulfill her mother's wishes. Soon after Harv had abandoned them, Lacy's mother had reverted back to her maiden name, Preston, and changed Lacy's last name as well.

At first, Lacy had carried the shame of her father's dishonesty and failures like a physical scar, but by high school, she had formed a new resolve. She would do what her father had failed to do—run a successful investment business, one that was clean and honest and thriving. From the moment she had made that decision as a teenager, Lacy had thrown herself into her schoolwork, striving for excellence.

Her work had paid off, leading to a full-ride scholarship for her undergraduate, a stint studying abroad in France, and finally obtaining an MBA from a prestigious university. Her mother had passed away before she had completed her MBA, and later she learned that her father had passed as well.

Being suddenly alone in the world could have broken her, but she wouldn't allow it. Instead, she had continued to push forward. Inside, she knew that she had made both herself and her mother proud. She had worked enormously hard for years to build her successful career, far away from her father's shameful scandals.

Her cell phone rang, pulling her from the rabbit hole of her thoughts and shattering the peaceful quiet of her apartment. Setting her wine glass aside, she strained to reach her phone, which she'd tossed at the other end of the couch and peered at the number on the screen. She didn't recognize it, but that wasn't too uncommon in her line of work. Often a pleased client would pass along her business cards to other business startups and advise them to get in touch with her.

Running her fingers through her honey-brown hair to get it out of her face, Lacy sat up straight and answered in her usual professional manner.

"Lacy Preston speaking. May I ask who is calling?"

"Ms. Preston, my name is Ronald Carp. I'm the

attorney for Nicholas Spielman's estate. I believe he was your grandfather?"

Lacy felt her mouth drop open, completely blindsided by the attorney's words. She sat frozen but her mind raced with the news that had been dropped like a live bomb into her well-ordered life.

"Ms. Preston?"

Lacy cleared her throat, tucking her knees up to her chest like a child and wrapping her arms around them as though holding herself together, but when she spoke she managed to keep her voice calm and steady.

"Yes, I'm here."

"I'm calling regarding your late grandfather's estate."

"Estate...?"

There was a pause on the other end of the line. "Were you unaware of Mr. Spielman's wishes?"

"My grandfather and I didn't have contact. I haven't spoken to him in over twenty years."

There was another pause. "I see," Mr. Carp said finally. "Well, then. Your grandfather owned property in Snowy Pine Ridge in New Hampshire. A rather extensive property, actually. I believe most would consider it a mansion, and it sits on several acres of land. He left it to you, Ms. Preston."

Lacy sat, stunned and aghast at the news, then her mouth thinned into a hard line. "I don't want it."

Mr. Carp cleared his throat. "Be that as it may, Ms. Preston, the property is legally yours."

Lacy dropped her head to rest against her knees and squeezed her eyes shut. She had spent most of her life running from the legacy of her father and grandfather. And now, a portion of that legacy was literally being forced upon her, whether she wanted it or not. And she most certainly, emphatically, deeply, did *not* want any part of it.

CHAPTER TWO

Derek Morse had been out on the snowy trails almost before the sun had risen, even though it was a Saturday morning. He didn't mind waking up early; in fact, there was something about being awake when everyone else around still slumbered on that brought him a sense of peace and clarity. The world could get so loud, even in his tiny hometown, and he took every chance he could get to immerse himself in the jaw-dropping scenery that made the small New Hampshire town of Snowy Pine Ridge a hidden gem.

Derek gave a low whistle, the signal his team of dogs all understood to mean that it was time to spring forward with extra energy. They threw themselves forward against their harnesses, pulling him on the dogsled with everything they had. He stood, legs wide on the runners, exulting in the brisk winter wind against his face as his team charged up the steep hill. The sled and the dogs' paws threw a steady spray of powdery snow behind them, and he found himself laughing aloud with the sheer joy of the moment.

Moments later, they crested the top of the hill, and Derek called for his team to stop. They slowed to a halt, their tongues lolling out of their open mouths and their panting breaths forming little puffy clouds in front of their faces. He reached forward, scratching the ears of the dog closest to him, Apollo. Apollo leaned into his hand, his tail wagging a mile a minute. Although that stretch of the trail with its long incline was difficult, he had trained his team well, and they tackled it with relative ease, something that always filled him with enormous pride.

"Good job, boy," he murmured, giving Apollo one last pat on the head before turning to look out at the vista spread below him.

Snowy Pine Ridge, with all its simple charms, lay below his gaze, and he soaked in the sight. This town was his whole world, the only place he had ever called home, and he didn't foresee that changing. In the distance, the spires of the church on the corner of Center Street and Main Street reached toward the sky, which had formed a cloudless blue in the early morning, belying the bitter cold temperatures.

The downtown area of town was filled with orderly streets, lined with adorable small shops and local businesses. The old iron clock in the town square, once black, had now weathered to a soft green, lending the square a stately charm. In the summertime, most of the shops had window boxes filled with flowers and leafy trees shading the cobblestone streets. Derek loved that time of year, but he loved winter even more, and not just because of his dogsledding business.

No, wintertime was when Snowy Pine Ridge showed herself to full advantage, at least in his opinion. Pine wreaths hung on shop doors and in shop windows, twinkly Christmas lights were strung on the trees in town and soft white snow rested on rooftops and formed gentle mounds along the sides of the streets. Often, during the evenings in December, old Christmas tunes would play over the speakers in the town square, or carolers would give small concerts in the open air.

You just can't find traditions and community like

that in a big city, Derek mused, taking in a lungful of crisp mountain air. *And you can't find views like this either.*

There had been a short time in his youth when he had wondered if he was a failure for not leaving his hometown, for not going to college like many of his friends, but he had long since let that go. Ever since he was a child, he had loved learning, but his favorite learning had always occurred outside of the classroom and out in nature. When he was only a little boy, his parents had signed him up for dogsled racing lessons, and he had taken to it like a fish to water. A retired dogsled racing champion, Cliff Morris, had settled in their town for its access to the best trails, and Derek's life had been sculpted by Cliff's decision.

Cliff had given Snowy Pine Ridge access to a unique sport, something not many towns could boast. When Derek was twenty-five, Cliff had decided to move out west to live closer to his children, leaving a void in the town. Derek, nervous but more sure than he'd ever been, knew that he wanted to continue carrying the torch of Cliff's legacy.

He had founded Winter Run Racing, his dogsledding business, and had worked it ever since.

Winter Run Racing was his whole life—-from raising and training his teams of dogs to giving lessons to organizing events to selling merchandise in his shop, Derek kept busy and loved every minute of it. His path had not been a traditional one, but he would not trade it for the world.

And none of it could have happened without the role models in my life, he thought. *Cliff Morris, you changed my life. And Nicholas Spielman, you did too.*

Nicholas Spielman had provided him with the loan that had financed Winter Run Racing's beginnings. The older man had looked over Derek's business proposal and taken a chance on him—something Derek was sure not many others would have. But Nicholas had seen potential in him and given him the loan, changing Derek's life forever.

Over the years, the men had become friends, and his passing had left a hole in Derek's heart. Nicholas had been a great man, always spreading his generosity and kindness through the town. Derek knew he wasn't the only person in town missing him.

"You are missed, Nicholas," Derek whispered, his words instantly whipped away by a winter wind that scoured across the ridge and shook the pine trees around him. "The world could use more men like you."

Turning back to his dogs, he moved down the line of them, giving each of them pats and murmuring to them softly. Their tails wagged, showing their readiness to get back to racing along the trails. They loved these excursions every bit as much as he did and, now that they had rested a bit, they were clearly itching to let loose their energy and race down another snowy trail.

Climbing back onto the sled he looked back out over the town one last time, breathing in the clean scent of the pines all around him and savoring the endorphins running through his system.

This is the life, he thought, taking it all in. Then, with a yip and a loud whistle, he sent his team surging forward once more, holding on tight and squinting against the morning sun as it glinted against the whiteness of the snow. *The sledding, the views, the scenery, the rush of racing... it just never gets old.*

Spontaneously, he threw his head back and let out a loud whoop, his exultant cry ringing through the crisp morning air.

* * *

"He left you a *mansion*?"

Lacy winced as her friend Madeline's squeal blared through the phone. Pulling her phone away from her ear and frowning, she hit the speaker button and set the phone on her bathroom counter.

"Yes, but as I said before, I don't want anything to do with it," Lacy reminded her.

She studied her expression in the mirror, dabbing on more of her expensive mud mask. Her green eyes stared back at her, more startling than usual because of the mask. Her honey-brown hair, which fell just above her shoulders in an A-line cut, was too short for a ponytail, so she'd swept it back with a headband. Satisfied that the mask fully covered her face, she leaned back to check her toenails, holding back her silk robe so she could see her feet.

With the stresses of her job, she had long since made self-care on Saturday mornings a priority. She wore toe separators to keep her freshly painted toenails from smudging. She'd painted her toenails crimson, her signature hue, and she saw with satisfaction that they were nearly dry. Grabbing her phone and padding carefully down the hallway, she poured herself a cup of coffee in the kitchen, adding a hazelnut creamer and inhaling its comforting aroma.

"Lacy, come *on*," Madeline was saying, and Lacy

could practically see her friend rolling her eyes. "Look, I know you've got some emotional baggage or whatever, but why would you turn your nose up at a free mansion?"

Lacy blew on her coffee then took a careful sip. "Because I didn't really know my grandfather and, even though he's gone, I don't relish the thought of taking a handout from a man who left my mother and me to fend for ourselves."

Madeline was quiet for a moment, but Lacy could hear the telltale sound of Madeline's manicured nails tapping. Madeline was a force of nature, always moving and unable to sit still. As a designer in the cutthroat and fast-paced world of fashion, Madeline was always bursting with ideas and the confidence to carry them out. She wasn't overly sentimental and, like Lacy, was entirely focused on getting ahead in her career. The two of them had bonded long ago, sensing in one another a kindred spirit. Many women their age were focused on getting married and having children, which had made making friends difficult. When Lacy met Madeline, she had been relieved to find another ambitious woman to join her circle of close friends.

"Maybe you need to reframe the issue," Madeline said, talking faster as she gathered steam.

"You specialize in investing. Why not look at this as another investment? It'll be a new asset to add to your portfolio."

"I hadn't considered that..."

"Well, you should! It only makes sense. Sure, you've got a less-than-happy history with your grandfather, but he's gone now and he left you a mansion. Why not get the most you can out of it? He owes you that much."

And more, Lacy thought, but she didn't voice the thought. The wheels in her head began turning with possibilities.

"I suppose I could go check it out and get some ideas," she said slowly.

"That's the spirit! You never know how you could use it to your benefit. You could sell it and take the profit, flip it into a venue, get someone to run it as a B&B... this whole inheritance thing has a ton of potential."

"You're right."

"And don't you forget it," Madeline teased. "Seriously, though, it's not like you have to move into the mansion and live in whatever dinky little town your grandfather settled in. All you have to do is check the property out and then make a plan from there."

Lacy took another sip of her coffee, mulling Madeline's words over in her mind. Madeline was not very sentimental, but she had made some good points. She had been letting old resentments and the turbulent emotions of her youth overcome her. Ronald Carp's phone call had been all she had thought about Friday, and it had made for a difficult day at her office. She'd thought her pain from the abandonment of her father and grandfather had long since been laid to rest, but it had reared its ugly head with a vengeance and plagued her thoughts since. Madeline's prosaic take on the situation had, in a way, been a breath of fresh air, and she finally felt like she was on familiar footing again. She knew the world of business and investments and walked through it with cool confidence, totally unlike the grieving little girl she had felt like the previous day.

"You're right," Lacy repeated again, her voice firmer now. "See, this is why I keep you around."

"That and free fashion advice."

Lacy laughed aloud at that, the sound surprising her. "And the free fashion advice," she agreed with a grin. "Okay, Madeline, you've convinced me—as soon as I wash off this mud mask I'm going to book a ticket to New Hampshire."

"There's the Lacy I know and love."

Lacy rose to her feet, anxious to get her plan started right away. "Thanks, Madeline. Talk soon, okay?"

"Call me when you get to New Hampshire. I've got your back."

CHAPTER THREE

Colette Hillis pried off her snow-covered boots in the back mudroom of her employer's house, grunting a little as her left boot refused to part with her foot. With one last mighty heave, the boot finally slid off, and she straightened up, blowing her hair out of her face. Now in stocking feet, she padded into the cozy, dated kitchen of Emma Cleaver's house. For the past several years, Colette had lived in the guesthouse on Emma's property and worked as her cook, cleaner, and companion.

In some ways, she felt like she and Emma had both rescued each other. Years ago, Colette had fled her hometown of Burlington as soon as she graduated high school, leaving behind a deeply troubled home life. Memories assaulted her, the way they still sometimes did when she least expected it—images of her alcoholic father, passed out on the couch with an empty liquor bottle beside him; her father screaming at her mother and punching a hole in the drywall; her mother packing up her things and moving out of the house, Colette in tow; her mother marrying a new man and building a new family where there wasn't quite space for Colette.

Colette tucked her blonde hair behind her ears, straightening her shoulders.

Not today, she thought fiercely. *That part of my life has been gone for years and years, and I never have to go back.*

She wrapped her arms around herself for a moment, closing her eyes and breathing in the familiar scent of Emma's house. After leaving Burlington, Colette had landed in Snowy Pine Ridge, lost and adrift. Emma had taken her in, offering her a home and employment, and the rest was history.

Over the years their relationship had changed from that of an employer and employee to that of a found family. And Colette knew it wasn't just charity—the elderly lady had never married and had no children, and she knew that Emma needed her just as much as Colette needed her.

The old wooden clock on the kitchen wall chimed softly and Colette automatically counted the chimes. Eight.

She had already known the time when she'd struggled through the snow to Emma's house, but the chiming of the clock every hour had become part of her routine, and Colette liked her routine. Stability and routine brought her peace, and there was peace in spades working for Emma Cleaver.

Walking over to the sink, she filled the coffee pot with water and got the pot percolating. Soon the kitchen would be filled with the comforting aromas of coffee and Emma would make an appearance, sniffing the air appreciatively the way she always did.

Humming softly to herself to banish the last of the unexpected memories from her past, Colette rummaged in the cabinet, pulling out the ingredients to make homemade waffles. Colette had perfected her recipe over the years, and now it was one of Emma's favorite breakfasts. The old lady had something of a sweet tooth, and she loved slathering them in rich, melted butter and drenching them in maple syrup. Colette had warned her time and again that she needed to cut back on the sweets, but Emma always smiled at her and told her that the sweet things in life made it worth living. So, Colette made sure Emma had her sweets, but she also took care to sneak healthier foods into Emma's diet.

Colette pulled on the drawer that held the spices, automatically giving it an extra yank since the drawer always stuck on the first pull, and rummaged around until she found the cinnamon. Cinnamon made her waffles sing, and she never made waffles without it. In no time at all, Colette was ladling batter onto the gridded waffle iron, the batter sizzling and popping as it hit the heated surface. She closed the iron, leaning against the counter and looking around the kitchen idly. Emma hadn't updated the house since she had bought it in the seventies, and it showed.

The yellow patterned linoleum on the floor was shockingly ugly, but somehow that made Colette love it more. The appliances, all once white, were now a faded cream color, but Emma refused to purchase new ones, stating firmly that 'they don't make 'em like they used to'.

Honestly, Colette was inclined to agree.

The old oven might be ugly as could be, but Colette knew all its quirks and it was still going strong. Across the kitchen, a worn and scarred wooden table sat beneath a huge picture window looking out at the backyard. A doily sat in the middle of the table, ceramic salt and pepper shakers in the shape of two cats playing resting atop it. Everything in the house had a history, but Colette loved it. To her, every faded, dated detail spoke of home and safety.

Hearing footsteps, Colette looked over to see Emma walking slowly down the hallway. The old woman paused in the kitchen doorway, closing her eyes and sniffing appreciatively, the way Colette had already known she would. Her pillowy white hair was gathered into a loose bun at the back of her head in a banana clip, and she wore a colorful chunky knitted cardigan.

"Something smells good," Emma said.

"The waffles will be ready in just a second," Colette replied, pulling a mug out of the cabinet and pouring a cup of coffee for Emma.

Emma patted Colette's cheek softly by way of thanks and took the proffered mug, carrying it over to the table and settling herself with a quiet grunt into her usual chair. She wrapped her wrinkled fingers around the mug for warmth, and Colette waited for Emma to say she wanted cream and lots of sugar, the way she always did, but Emma sat silent. Emma stared out the window, clearly lost in thought as she stared at the snowy landscape.

Silently, Colette set the container of sugar and the pitcher of cream on the table in front of her employer.

As she returned to her station at the waffle iron, Colette kept an eye on Emma. "Did you sleep well?"

"Oh, about as well as an old lady like me can. I woke up sometime before dawn and tossed and turned until it was time to get up."

"Maybe it's time to see about getting you a new pillow or mattress."

"Dear, at my age, sleeping through the night is a rarity." Emma took a sip of her coffee, pulling a face when she realized she hadn't added creamer or sugar yet. "Is the guesthouse staying warm enough? I don't know how you sleep out there."

"It's plenty warm, I promise. The wood stove keeps it nice and toasty. Besides, you know I sleep with two of your handmade quilts."

Emma nodded, lapsing once more into silence. She turned her head and stared out the window, resting her chin in one hand. Colette studied her, noting the way Emma slumped, as though too weary to hold herself up. Emma was getting on in years, but she usually had a good amount of energy and vim, but that was missing this morning. Instead, Emma's eyes looked watery and careworn. Colette set a plate with two waffles stacked on it in front of Emma, then sat down across from her.

"Emma, is everything all right?"

Emma's lips turned down and she began buttering her waffle, moving with an exhausted slowness. "Oh, don't mind me, dear. I have been thinking about the past." She mustered up a smile that didn't reach her tired eyes. "Old women like me have plenty of time to reminisce."

Colette poured some syrup on her own waffle, waiting for Emma to continue. When Emma lifted her fork to take a bite of her syrup-less waffle, Colette knew something was really wrong. She reached out and gently lowered Emma's hand, pushing the bottle of maple syrup toward the older woman, who blinked a little. When Emma made no move toward it, Colette poured the syrup for her.

"Have you been thinking about anything specific?" Colette asked. "In all this reminiscing?"

Emma took a thoughtful bite, once more staring out the window. In the spring it was a riot of colorful flowers and lovely garden beds that Colette helped Emma maintain, but for now it was white as far as the eye could see with mounds of powdery snow.

"I am happy with my life," Emma said suddenly. "I am, truly."

Colette waited, knowing that if she stayed quiet, Emma would likely tell her more in her own time. A moment later, her patience was rewarded.

"My life has been a quiet one, as you know very well. I never married, but I did find love." Emma reached out and patted Colette's hand. "I never had any children to keep me company in my old age, but I was fortunate enough to meet you, dear. You've become like a daughter to me."

Colette smiled, her heart swelling with love. "I'm grateful for our relationship too. You mean the world to me."

Emma patted her hand again, returning her smile. Just then, the sound of bells jingling caught their attention and they looked out the window to see Derek on his sled, pulled by his team of dogs, sliding to a stop in the backyard. Emma perked up at the sight of him, the way she always did, and waved at him through the window. Derek waved back and his dogs jumped and yipped in the fresh morning air. Derek made it a habit to drive the team through the backyard whenever he was close by so that Emma could have a look at the team from her window, and the older lady always looked forward to his visits. Emma gave him another wave and blew him a kiss.

Colette jumped to her feet and raced into the

mudroom, stuffing her feet into her boots. Not bothering with a coat, she raced out the back door, wrapping her arms around herself for some warmth. Derek was her cousin, and he was a big part of the reason she had chosen Snowy Pine Ridge when she'd left Burlington for good after high school.

"Derek!" she called, waving to get his attention.

Derek hopped off the sled and walked to her. "It's freezing out here, Col! You're crazy to come out here without a coat."

"I know," Colette replied with a shiver. The bitter wind stung her cheeks and whipped her hair into her eyes. "Can you come in for a second? I want to talk to you, and I'm sure Emma would love to see you too."

"I can't right now. I was out for a quick morning ride, but I'm headed back to the shop to give some lessons. I'll come by for a proper visit later when I don't have the team with me."

Colette bit her lip, wondering if she was overreacting to Emma's depressed mood.

"What's wrong? Is Emma okay?"

"That's the thing—I don't know. She's been very... contemplative... this morning. Maybe not sad exactly? More nostalgic?"

Derek grinned at her. "I'm sure it's fine. We all

have days when we're lost in our thoughts a little bit. It's nothing to worry about."

"I hope so..."

Derek headed back to his team, throwing a cheerful grin over his shoulder to her. "Seriously, don't worry, Colette! I'll be back to see Emma as soon as I can, okay?"

Colette nodded, mustering up a smile. By now she was trembling continually from the cold.

Derek hopped onto the sled and gave Emma one more wave before turning back to Colette. "Col, I'm sure she's okay," he said, then gave her a scolding look. "Now, get back inside before you freeze to death."

Colette took his advice, hurrying back into the house. As she shut the back door behind her and took in a breath of the warm air from the kitchen, Colette glanced back at Emma, who was once more staring listlessly out the window.

I hope Derek is right, she thought, worry filling her again. *I really hope he's right.*

CHAPTER FOUR

"Keep the change," Lacy told the cab driver, handing him some cash. "I don't need any help with my bags."

She'd had to take a taxi from a town nearly forty minutes away. Apparently her late grandfather's tiny town was a good distance from the nearest airport, and the cab fare was staggeringly high.

This whole thing better be worth it, she thought, feeling grumpy.

She generally didn't mind flying, but in snagging a last-minute flight she'd had to fly economy and the man sitting beside her had hogged the armrest and tried to hit on her multiple times, despite the fact that she'd opened a novel and turned herself away from him as much as possible. She also hadn't eaten much, aside from the packet of pretzels on the plane, and her stomach was protesting angrily by now.

The driver thanked her, pocketing the money and waiting while she climbed out of the cab, her carry-on suitcase and purse in tow. A light snow was drifting down in the dimming light of the sunset.

Her heeled boots sank into the snow on the sidewalk and she hurried toward the shop just ahead with the name "Martinez Real Estate" stenciled in its window. Ronald Carp had given her the name of one Matthew Martinez, telling her that he was in possession of the deed and the keys to the mansion.

Lacy shivered, holding her coat against her more tightly. She had thought she was pretty used to the cold, living in the midwest, but the New Hampshire winter was something else entirely. The bitter wind sliced through her peacoat, and she breathed a sigh of relief as the warm air inside the shop greeted her.

A gust of wind slammed the door shut behind her and she jumped a little. A stocky man with sandy curls emerged from a back room, his eyebrows raised. His blue eyes crinkled at the corners as he smiled and hurried toward her, his hand extended.

"You must be Lacy Preston," he said, shaking her hand. "Ronald called and told me to expect you."

"And you must be Matthew Martinez. Thanks for meeting with me."

"Not at all! Glad to be of help in whatever way I can. I'm assuming this is your first time to Snowy Pine Ridge?"

Lacy nodded. "It is."

"Beautiful, isn't it?"

"I didn't see much," she admitted. "I was going over emails on my phone in the taxi up here."

"Well, then. You have a treat when you wake up tomorrow!"

Lacy smiled, charmed by his vivacious, open demeanor. "I'm sure I will."

"Let's sit," Matthew said. "I'm sure you have a lot of questions."

A large desk covered in rolled up floor plans and schematics for buildings, nearly hiding an aging computer, took up a good portion of the room. Matthew settled himself at the desk, gesturing for her to sit in one of the mismatched chairs across from him. He swept some of the papers aside, bracing his elbows against the desk and leaning toward her. His direct gaze bored into her eyes, disarming her a little.

"I'm so sorry for your loss, Ms. Preston. We all loved Nicholas around here."

"Call me Lacy," she replied automatically,

choosing to ignore the reference to her grandfather. "I appreciate you keeping your office open for me so we could meet tonight."

Matthew waved that away. "I work all hours, honestly. There are some nights I end up falling asleep at my desk when I get too wrapped up in a project." His eyes lit up with excitement. "For instance, there's a house I'm flipping right now, and I've been working up a new layout for it since I'm thinking of knocking out a few walls to create an open floor plan." He trailed off, seeming to realize he was rambling. "Sorry, I get too excited about my work."

"I feel the same way about my career. No need to apologize." Lacy sat forward a little. "I *would* like to get down to brass tacks, though, if you wouldn't mind."

"Absolutely. Let me fill you in on some of the specifics." Matthew dug through the mound on his desk and pulled out a stack of papers for her. "I've pulled the tax records for the house, which are public record, but you'll have to go to city hall to get blueprints of the house and whatnot."

"That's fine."

"Before you see the house, I think I should warn you—as Nicholas got older, he had a hard time taking care of the house, and it already needed repairs when he bought it. I'm not sure if he had the funds to make the repairs he always talked about."

Lacy bit back an unladylike snort and resisted the urge to roll her eyes. Of course her grandfather hadn't maintained the mansion. That would fit in with what she knew about him. A man who made shady business deals wasn't likely to care for a historical home the way it deserved. Besides, if the house was falling down around his ears, he deserved to live in that decay and disarray. Men who abandon their families didn't deserve better, at least in her opinion.

"Let me guess," Lacy said, her voice dry. "It's a tumbling down shack."

"No, no," Matthew was quick to assure her. "The mansion is beautiful, and it's full of history." He sat back, rubbing his chin. "You'll see what I mean when you see the architectural details on it—it's a gem for sure. It just needs some work to make it livable. Of course, that's assuming you want to live there."

"I haven't decided what I'll be doing with it yet. That's why I'm here."

"Of course, of course. It has lots of potential, but it definitely needs some TLC to bring it back to full glory. I know for certain that some of the plumbing needs to be reworked—old pipes and all that, and I'm sure the furnace needs to be replaced."

Lacy sighed. "Unsurprising." She tapped one manicured fingernail against his desk, thinking. "Can we take a look tonight?"

"The sun has already set," Matthew pointed out. "I think your best bet is to look tomorrow. I do have the keys and the deed for you, though."

Lacy accepted the items from him. "Do you think you could draw me a map to his house?"

"Absolutely."

Matthew quickly sketched out a map, pointing out landmarks for her. She studied it, nodding as he spoke.

"This looks perfect. Thank you, Matthew."

Lacy rose, shaking his hand again. "I've got a room booked at The Snowy Pine. Is it far from here?"

"It's just a block up the road, heading toward the town square. You can't miss it."

Lacy thanked him again, then wished him a good night. Matthew waved a goodbye at her, already turning back to the mountain of work on his desk as she slipped out the door of the shop. Night had fully fallen during her conversation with Matthew, taking with it the last illusion of warmth the sun could offer.

She wheeled her suitcase behind her, dragging it over hardened clumps of icy snow and trying to keep from slipping on slick patches of sidewalk. To her relief, The Snowy Pine hotel was as close as Matthew had told her.

The hotel sat back from the road a bit, and even in her haste Lacy couldn't help but notice the welcoming New England cottage look of it all. Exposed wooden rafters and a large polished wooden staircase welcomed her in the large front hall, reminding her forcefully of the inn featured in *White Christmas*. A friendly older woman welcomed her, checking her in and handing her a room key. Lacy couldn't help but smile when the woman told her that a tray of hot cocoa and freshly baked cookies were waiting for her in her room.

As much as I'm prepared to hate this town, I can't pretend that I'm not already head over heels in love with this hotel. This is like something straight out of a Christmas movie, Lacy thought, admiring her surroundings as she climbed the stairs and made her way to her bedroom.

After unlocking the door, she was greeted by the promised cocoa and cookies sitting on a tray. A large homemade quilt covered the queen-sized four-poster bed, and a rocking chair sat beside an original fireplace in the corner. Thick rugs covered the old hardwood floors and a delicate floral wallpaper made the room feel cozy and feminine.

Lacy set her suitcase down, taking off her coat and drinking in the room. If she was going to have to deal with the ghosts of her grandfather and her past, she couldn't have asked for a homier place to do it.

She picked up the mug of hot cocoa, settling herself into the rocking chair and looking out the window over the landscape. Even in the dark, the snow made it appear lighter out than it was. She took a sip, savoring the sweet warmth as it rolled over her tongue.

As she sat, her mind kept jumping ahead to her grandfather's mansion. She had come so far and it was so near. The thought of waiting until the next morning suddenly seemed impossible to her. She had never been one to leave for tomorrow what could be done right away and, with sudden decision, she pulled her coat back on. Pausing only to grab the map and the keys to the mansion, Lacy slipped back out into the night.

Her fashionable city clothes were no match for the New Hampshire cold, and she began to question the prudence of her spontaneous decision as the wind bit at her cheeks and snow worked its way into her boots as her feet sank deeper than she'd planned into snowdrift after snowdrift. Setting her jaw with determination, Lacy tucked her chin lower into the collar of her peacoat and hunched against the wind, trudging doggedly forward. Cold minutes passed, but eventually she found the street that led to Nicholas Spielman's mansion.

The mansion loomed large and formless in the dark, only taking shape as she trudged up the long tree-lined driveway and got closer. To her surprise, the house was far more beautiful than she'd expected. The Victorian-style mansion was sprawled with turrets, bay windows, a wraparound porch, and artistically detailed woodwork. Other, less beautiful details, quickly forced themselves on her attention as she got closer.

One of the front windows was broken, missing several panes of glass, and had been inexpertly repaired with cardboard and duct tape. Some of the shutters were broken, hanging off their hinges at crazy angles. The woodwork, which must have once been beautifully and colorfully painted, was peeling and worn.

And that's just the exterior, she thought. *I'm sure the interior is in a sorry state as well.*

She struggled up the front steps, yelping when a

rotted board gave way beneath and shifting her weight just in time. A large fallen branch blocked the top step, and she grunted as she clambered over it, almost falling in the process. Gritting her teeth, she bit back a curse of annoyance.

"Couldn't be bothered to maintain this house," she muttered, her early grumpiness flaring again. "I'm not surprised, though."

Fumbling with the keys, her fingers stiff with the cold, she finally managed to open the front door. The house was just as cold inside as it was outside, which was to be expected. She tapped blindly at the wall, searching for a light switch. Her fingers finally found one and she flipped it, but nothing happened. With a sigh, she realized that the electricity must have been shut off. Using her teeth, she pulled off one of her leather gloves and then fished her phone from her pocket, turning on its flashlight function.

The light from her phone illuminated a large entryway with a grand, curving staircase. Dust motes floated softly through the air. A large sitting room opened to her right and she crept in, suddenly feeling the need to be quiet.

There was something slightly haunting about walking through the rooms that her own grandfather had so recently inhabited, and she caught herself holding her breath. She moved slowly through the room, studying the beautiful crown molding, the grand fireplace with its sooty marble mantelpiece. There was something romantic, almost magical, about the home, even though she did find it a little haunting in the nighttime.

A large, well-worn armchair rested beside the fireplace, a book sitting open on its seat, as though its occupant was about to return. Out of curiosity, she picked up the book—*Crime and Punishment*, by Dostoevsky.

Interesting choice, Grandfather, she mused, making a wry face.

She set the book aside and continued exploring the main floor of the house, deciding that the upstairs could wait for morning. She chided herself for being a little afraid, but the dark upper floors felt too spooky to take on without the benefit of the sun's safety. The kitchen revealed itself to be dated and cluttered and, sure enough, it looked like there was some water damage on the walls. That would certainly require the work of a skilled contractor.

A light flashed in the distance outside the kitchen window and she jumped a little, hurrying to the window to peer out into the night. The light blinked out of sight and then, a few seconds later, blinked back into view. She frowned, puzzled, and hurried down the hall and out of the front door, wanting to investigate. She locked the door behind her and made her way carefully down the stairs before turning around the corner of the house to look for the light again.

Just as she turned the corner, the light appeared again, this time closer. She strained her ears, thinking she heard the sound of bells in the air. The light blinked out again, blocked by the crest of a small hill just behind the house. She walked toward it, her curiosity now fully alive. The sound of bells was getting louder. Lacy held her coat around her tightly, squinting against the icy wind and searching for the curiously moving light.

Suddenly a pack of dogs burst over the crest of the hill, followed instantly by the light, which was now so bright it nearly blinded her. The dogs barreled toward her and Lacy had no time to move. Her arms flew in front of her face to protect herself, a scream ripping itself from her lungs.

CHAPTER FIVE

Derek gripped the handles of the sled hard, yelling a command for his team to stop. With teeth gritted and working with all his might to maintain his balance, the sled swerved to the side as the dogs dug their paws into the snow, skidding to an abrupt halt, spraying a shower of snow over the lone figure illuminated by the lantern attached to the sled. Derek's breaths came in hard puffs as he slowly let go of the handles and stared at the woman, their eyes locked for the space of several long heartbeats.

As the adrenaline began to fade from his system, his lagging mind caught back up to the present and he finally took in the figure standing frozen in the lamplight. He didn't recognize her, which meant she likely wasn't from town—as though her woefully inadequate winter coat and lack of hat or scarf wasn't already evidence of that. Her mouth still hung open slightly, though she had stopped screaming, and her chest heaved with breaths. One leather-gloved hand clutched at her throat and tendrils of her short brown hair whipped wildly around her flushed face in the wind.

Derek knew he would need to check on the woman, but first he needed to calm his team. They were antsy and restless, clearly anxious to get moving again. This was one of his younger teams, still wet behind the ears and not experienced enough for his students to use for lessons. As such, they needed all the extra practice and training he could give them, which was why he had chosen to squeeze in an extra trail run that night. Most folks were home for the night by now, and he had certainly not expected to find anyone near Nicholas Spielman's vacant mansion.

"Shh, shh," he soothed one of the more nervous of his pups, patting its head and crouching beside it to look into its eyes. "Calm down, buddy."

The dog whined a little but stopped its nervous trotting after a few more moments. Satisfied, Derek gave him one last pat and then stood, walking toward the woman. She had closed her mouth now, but still stared at him with wide eyes full of shock and utter confusion. If she was from out of town the last thing she had likely expected to see coming at her in the darkness was a sled pulled by a team of dogs. Sure, it was a common sight in Snowy Pine Ridge, but their town was the exception and he knew it.

He stopped within a foot or so of her, startled by how vividly green her eyes were, even illuminated only in the lantern light and the waning moon overhead. She lifted her chin at his approach, her green eyes suddenly snapping fire, a belated stress response to the traumatic experience she had just undergone. He hoped that he had not terrified her too badly, but he had seen enough to know that she had likely had the scare of her life. His team of dogs was friendly as could be, but how would a stranger know that when a pack of dogs suddenly careened at them out of the dark?

"Ma'am, I'm so—"

Those few words were all he managed before she lit into him. Apparently, his voice was the last impetus she needed to recover from her shock enough to act.

"What in the WORLD were you thinking?" she yelled, jabbing a finger at his face. "You could have killed me! Do you have any idea how... how *reckless* that was?" She gestured wildly around him, encompassing him and his team for good measure. "What if you hadn't stopped in time? How many other people have you almost killed?!"

Derek lifted his hands as a sign of peace, waiting for her to cool down enough to listen. She stared at him, her mouth tight and her eyes raining down fire at him. A detached part of his mind wondered how such a tiny package could hold so much spitfire, but he made sure to keep that comment to himself. He was sure she wouldn't appreciate the observation, or the fact that she looked less authoritative and frightening during her tirade than she did like an adorable baby tiger trying to frighten off a larger predator.

"Ma'am," he tried again, keeping his voice neutral and calm and, with a mighty effort, holding back the smile that threatened to curl up the corners of his mouth. She would just think he was laughing at her, and he had no intention of adding insult to injury. "Please let me apologize for scaring you like that."

The woman folded her arms, some of the fight going out of her. "All right then, apologize."

Derek raised an eyebrow and found that he had to work even harder now to muscle back the smile that threatened to make its appearance. He cleared his throat. "I'm sorry we scared you, and I'm glad you're all right." He hesitated, then continued on, keeping his tone polite but matter-of-fact. "You should know that most folks around here know better than to wander far from the streetlights in town without some form of illumination. You know, a headlamp or a flashlight or something."

The woman pulled her head back, her brow furrowing. "Why in the world would I carry a headlamp with me?"

"It's a basic rule for living safely around here. I'm guessing you're not from this town."

The woman drew herself up, looking affronted and Derek waited for her to start off on another tirade. To his surprise, though, she loosened her folded arms and let out a sigh that ended in a sheepish laugh. "It's that obvious, huh?"

"Kind of," he admitted. "I really am sorry we scared you. Hopefully we didn't sour you on Snowy Pine Ridge. We don't usually scare our visitors half to death like that."

The woman pulled a wry face. "Trust me, I was already a little sour about this place even before that near-death experience. I never expected to find myself in a remote place like this of my own accord."

Derek eyed her. *There's definitely a story behind a statement like that,* he thought.

He didn't even know this woman, but he was already curious to hear just what it was that had made her set her heart against the little New Hampshire town that made up his whole world.

And I don't even know her name, he realized.

"I'm Derek Morse," he offered, reaching out to shake her hand. "I figured you might need my name when you file a police report for attempted murder."

It pleased him to no end when the woman laughed aloud at his lame joke, and he liked the way her laugh transformed her face from the anger she had worn before. She shook his hand firmly, and he sensed immediately that she was in the habit of carrying herself confidently through the world.

"Lacy Preston."

"Well, Lacy, let me officially welcome you to our town. Now that we're acquainted, can I ask what had you skulking around the outskirts of town?"

"I wasn't *skulking,*" Lacy protested, then broke off when she realized he was teasing her again. She huffed and rolled her eyes, but she couldn't help but smile. "Not that it's any of your business, but if you must know, I just inherited this house." She paused, tilting her head and throwing him a look filled with challenge. "Which means I also own the property we're standing on. Wouldn't that mean I should file a police report for attempted murder *and* trespassing?"

Her quick wit brought out a bark of surprised laughter from him, which sent his dogs baying and barking into the night air as well. He glanced over his shoulder at them, quieting them with a quick order, and turned back to face her. Her unexpected admission had brought with it even more questions about who she was and what had brought her to town.

"This mansion belonged to Nicholas Spielman," he replied slowly, searching her face for any resemblance to his late friend, but finding none. "Are you family?"

"I'm his granddaughter," she said, her voice dry and holding a hint of tartness. "He didn't choose to be a part of my life before this, so I don't know why he left it to me, but I can't very well just reject it. So. Here I am."

Derek blinked, a little overwhelmed by her words. She had clipped them off casually, as though speaking about a mild annoyance, but he sensed from the suddenly closed-off look in her eyes that painful baggage from the past lurked in what she'd said. Nicholas had never talked about his family, apart from his son, Harv. He had questions for her now, many more, but he held his tongue. He had no right to ask about her seemingly complicated relationship with her grandfather, so he opted for a safer route.

"What do you think of the house?"

Lacy glanced over her shoulder at it automatically and shrugged. "It's certainly seen better days. I can already tell it will take a mountain of work if it's going to pass muster."

"Muster for what?"

"That, I haven't decided yet."

Derek considered the mansion, trying to see it through her eyes instead of through the filter of his fond memories of Nicholas. "It definitely needs work, but I promise it's less spooky in the daylight."

Lacy pulled another wry face. "We'll see about that," was all she said, and he wondered if she had already looked around inside the house before their run-in.

Before he could ask her more about her thoughts on the house, his dogs started baying again, setting up a racket that let him know in no uncertain terms that they were good and ready to hit the trails again. Derek shook his head, a little exasperated but also amused. Lacy caught his look and smiled a little, studying his team with some interest.

"I knew dogsledding was a thing, but I didn't think it *actually* existed in the real world," she admitted suddenly.

"It very much *is* a thing, especially here in Snowy Pine Ridge." He quieted his dogs again, this time walking over to pet them and murmur some reassurances. "This team is still pretty young, and they haven't quite learned how to control their excitement."

Lacy bent down beside the lead dog, Max, and let him sniff her hand. When his tail began wagging happily she scratched him behind the ears and smiled as he melted into her touch.

"He likes you."

Lacy looked up. "He's pretty adorable. You know, now that he's not careening toward my face at top speed."

"Touché."

Lacy shivered and Derek suddenly realized she must be freezing in her peacoat, especially now that her adrenaline had likely worn off. He was perfectly cozy in his winter gear, but she looked like she might turn into a popsicle at any moment, and he doubted she was staying in the vacant house behind them.

"Are you staying in town?"

She nodded. "At The Snowy Pine."

"Can I give you a lift back?"

Lacy stood, eying the small sled with a skeptical look, her cheeks flushing a little, and he wondered if she was realizing that she would have to stand in the circle of his arms to ride in front of him. It was no different than riding on a motorcycle with someone, but from the way her jaw was setting in a mulishly stubborn way, he already knew what her answer was going to be.

"On that thing? Not a chance."

Derek lifted his hands again by way of a peace offering. "I wasn't trying to be forward or make you uncomfortable. It's a cold night and it's a long walk back to the inn."

"Mr. Morse, I am perfectly capable of taking care of myself," she said severely, drawing herself up to her full height, which wasn't much.

Derek stepped back, giving her a nod and finding himself hiding another amused smile. "Suit yourself, Ms. Preston," he replied, mimicking her formality.

He climbed back onto his sled and whistled. The dogs broke into a run and surged forward, leaving Lacy Preston behind. He shook his head as they plunged back onto the dark, snowy trail, making their way back toward Winter Run Racing. As he rode, his thoughts returned again and again to the woman he had just met.

Only a very, very determined woman would pick a walk in the dark through unfamiliar territory just to prove a point, he thought.

An amused smile lifted the corners of his mouth once more.

CHAPTER SIX

Lacy took what she felt must have been her first full breath of the day as she made the trek back to her grandfather's house.

Well, my house now, she reminded herself just as a clump of wet snow slid off a branch overhead and landed with a wet plop on her shoulder. She brushed it off and tossed a glare at the branch. *Typical for this town.*

It wasn't enough that she had almost been run over by a dogsled team the night before. No, now even the trees were out to get her. As soon as the thought ran across her mind, Lacy had to stifle a laugh at how ridiculous it sounded.

Chalk it up to not enough sleep and too much upheaval lately.

Continuing her walk toward the house, Lacy tucked her chin further into her coat against the cold. She had felt like a marshmallow while getting dressed that morning as she'd layered on a long-sleeve shirt beneath the warmest sweater she'd packed and pulled fleece-lined tights on beneath her jeans. It may not have shown when she looked in the mirror, but she felt as though she'd gained twenty pounds. Now, though, in the freezing winter wonderland that was New Hampshire, she was grateful for the extra layers.

As she turned the next street corner, the house appeared up ahead, set back from the road by an expansive lawn and the tree-lined drive that, even in winter, looked stunning and grand. The house sat on the edge of town, its backyard melting seamlessly into the New Hampshire forest.

Which, of course, is exactly what provided one Derek Morse and his team of dogs the ability to fly out of the night like bats from hell and nearly run me over, she thought, pulling a wry face. *Apparently easy access to the trails around here means this house sits in a danger zone.*

With her boot, she nudged at the ruts Derek's sled had left in the snow by the side of the house, her face warming a little as she remembered the events of the previous night. She may have been scared out of her wits, but she had to admit that there was something intriguing about a man with such a rugged hobby.

It was a far cry from some of the men in St. Louis. Just last month, she had gone on a date with a man who rambled on about his obsession for virtual golf. Only good manners had kept Lacy from getting up and walking out. There had not been a second date, that was for sure.

Realizing she was comparing Derek, a man she barely knew, with men she had dated in St. Louis, Lacy shook her head slightly, as though to clear her head and turned away from the dogsled tracks with a resolute air.

Squaring her shoulders, she turned and looked at the house, giving it a real once-over for the first time now that she had the light of day to assist her. Derek and his team were soon forgotten as she studied the rambling Victorian mansion. As much as she hated to think her grandfather had good taste, she had to admit that, underneath all the layers of neglect and needed repairs, she could see how the place could have captured the old man's heart.

Her eyes traveled over the gingerbread trim and up one of the turrets, catching on a small stained-glass window, so delicate and beautiful her breath caught in her throat at the sight of it.

Don't let the charm of this place fool you, she reminded herself as she tromped up the snowy front porch steps and pulled the key from her pocket. *This place still needs a mountain of work, and you still haven't figured out what to do with it.*

The mansion was large, she had already gathered that much, which meant that maybe she could flip it into a B&B. Even as the thought occurred to her, she wondered if anyone would even stay there, what with the adorable and cozy inn just a few minutes away in the heart of town.

Or maybe I could use it as a venue, she thought, pushing open the front door, which stuck a little. *Of course, the rooms might be too small for that.*

The little she'd seen of the house last night had shown that the main floor was made up of many smaller rooms rather than an open floor plan, in true Victorian fashion.

This might be harder than I thought...

Catching herself beginning to feel overwhelmed and dismayed, Lacy forced herself not to spiral into negative thoughts. She never allowed herself to think that way in her business dealings. Confidence and gumption were required in her line of work, and she simply needed to view this house as another one of her projects. Lacy Preston had never been one to back down from a challenge, and she wasn't about to start now.

Even if this mansion brought with it unwelcome reminders of the grandfather she had barely known and the father who had abandoned her. She vowed then and there, while standing in the grand foyer, that she would not let this project defeat her.

Squaring her shoulders and setting her chin, Lacy pulled her phone from her pocket and opened the Notes app. Methodically, moving from room to room, she spent the next several hours studying every detail of the house and taking notes of what needed to be fixed. The list in her phone grew longer and longer as she noted peeling wallpapers that needed to be stripped and replaced, squealing door hinges that needed oil, broken window panes, the scuffed and scarred wooden floors.

She would need to get an official inspection to check on the state of the plumbing and electrical work too. And, of course, the entire place needed a deep clean, which meant a mountain of cleaning supplies just to excavate the beauty and character that she could already see waiting to burst forth once the house was given some TLC.

Hours later, Lacy tucked her phone back into her pocket and stretched, taking a long inhale through her nose and immediately sneezing from all the dust in the air. Laughing in spite of herself, Lacy made her way down the stairs from the third floor, where she had been poking around in the nooks and crannies, back to the grand foyer.

Her stomach grumbled loudly, reminding her that the muffin she'd scarfed down at The Snowy Pine that morning had been woefully inadequate for the hours of work she had just put in assessing every inch of the house. Satisfied with her morning's progress and refusing to think about the fact that assessing the needs of the house was the easiest of all the work to come, Lacy locked the front door and headed back into town.

She wandered down the sidewalk of the main street, weaving her way through the Christmas shoppers and townsfolk going about their business, until a bakery caught her eye. Decadent pastries displayed in the window with the words "Sweet Thing Bakery" stenciled on it set her stomach growling once more, but it was the mouth-watering aromas of freshly-baked bread and goodies that made the decision for her. Pulling open the quaint wooden front door that made a little bell jingle to announce her presence, Lacy stepped into a wonderland of baked goods.

The bakery's interior, quaint and adorable, made her pause. She was greeted by white shiplap walls, one of which held a large hand-painted menu detailing all that the bakery had to offer. Along the wall of picture windows, vintage wooden booths painted a distressed powdery blue held several patrons, sipping coffee and eating.

The crowning feature, though, was an old-fashioned polished wooden counter that ran almost the length of one wall.

It held a variety of glass-domed cake stands, each piled high with sugary confections. Lacy's mouth watered at the sight of golden-brown gingerbread men, sugar cookies covered in the most delicate and intricate frosting work she'd ever seen, frosted red velvet brownies, enormous cinnamon rolls covered in a sugary glaze...

"Welcome! How can I help you?"

Lacy tore her gaze away from the seemingly endless row of sweet treats to look at the woman standing behind the counter, waiting to take her order. The woman, who Lacy guessed was in her mid-twenties, had thick blonde hair pulled back in a perky high ponytail that bounced and swung whenever she moved, which was a lot. She wore a huge smile and had bright eyes, exuding a welcoming aura that instantly set Lacy at ease.

She looks exactly like the kind of person that makes treats for a living, Lacy thought with some amusement.

"I'm in desperate need of a coffee," Lacy replied with a smile. "I saw a peppermint mocha on the menu that sounds divine."

"You're going to *love* it," the woman replied, then clapped her hands as an idea occurred to her. "And my peppermint chocolate scone would be perfect with it! Let me get you one, on the house!"

Lacy blinked, stunned and a little overwhelmed at the flow of words, but she wasn't going to turn down a free scone. "Thank you, wow. That's so kind of you."

The woman waved away her thanks, beaming as she placed the scone on a plate and began preparing Lacy's coffee. "I'm Sarah, by the way. Sarah Langston. I know pretty much everyone in town, which means you're new. Are you visiting?"

By now, Lacy had begun to get used to Sarah's effusive, bubbly manner, and she took those frank observations in stride.

"Lacy Preston. And yes, I'm just visiting."

"That's wonderful!" Sarah added a generous spiral of whipped cream to the top of Lacy's coffee and pushed it toward her. "I hope you'll love it here —Snowy Pine Ridge is a special place."

"I'm beginning to see that," Lacy admitted, taking a sip of her peppermint mocha and sighing with pleasure. She pulled out her credit card and handed it to Sarah.

"May I ask what brings you to town? I don't want to pry, of course!"

"No, no, you're fine." Lacy took another sip of her mocha, deciding not to hedge. "Nicholas Spielman was my grandfather, and he left me his house. I'm here to figure out what to do with it."

Sarah handed back her card, her smile dimming for a moment. "I'm so sorry for your loss. We all loved Nicholas around here, you know." She twirled her ponytail around her finger for a moment and sighed. "He was such a good man."

It was only with great effort that Lacy kept herself from raising her eyebrows in obvious disbelief, so she hid her discomfort by taking a bite of her scone, buying herself some time. Luckily, Sarah continued talking without noticing and offered some more information about the man Lacy knew nothing about.

"He and Harv really brought this town to life—but I'm sure I don't have to tell you that—by helping so many of us get loans and financing to open our businesses. This main street used to look a lot different. You know, a lot of empty buildings and all that. With Harv and Nicholas's help, a lot of us got to live out our dreams of opening our own businesses. I wouldn't have my bakery if it weren't for their help." Sarah looked at Lacy, her eyes soft. "They sure left a hole in this town when they passed, and not just because we miss their help with investment and loans."

Lacy murmured something unintelligible by way of response, but her mind was spinning. Everything Sarah had said went against what her mother had told her of Harv and Nicholas. Her mother had taken pains to tell her, over and over again, how the two men's shady business practices had led to Harv's bankruptcy and subsequent abandonment of his family.

Could her mother have been wrong? Lacy had never looked into the bankruptcy herself, taking her mother's word for it...

No, Lacy reprimanded herself, stopping the agitated thoughts before they could take over. *Harv and Nicholas must have fooled everyone around here.*

That's all there is to it. I bet if I dug around and looked closer, I'd find evidence of something rotten below the surface.

"Lacy? Are you okay?"

Lacy blinked a little and met Sarah's gaze, plastering a smile on her face. "Yes! I was just... thinking about buying a piece of ginger cake instead of going back to the inn for lunch. Why not? Calories on trips don't count, right?" Lacy stopped, realizing she probably sounded a bit hysterical, but Sarah didn't seem to notice, much to Lacy's relief.

"You can't go wrong with my ginger cake," Sarah agreed, all enthusiasm once again. She leaned forward, winking conspiratorially. "In my bakery, calories don't count *ever*."

Lacy laughed. "In that case, I'll be eating all my 'meals' here."

Sarah was just about to grab a piece of cake for Lacy when the bell on the door jingled and a gust of cold air blew in. "Derek! Good to see you," Sarah called over, waving.

Lacy, who had turned automatically when she heard the door, froze a little as Derek walked in.

She had known he was tall from the previous night, but that had been the extent of things. Now, in broad daylight, she was taken aback by how absurdly good-looking he was. His thick auburn hair, windblown and unruly, framed a tan face, evidence of his outdoor work. A smattering of freckles crossed his fine, straight nose, but what Lacy noticed most of all was his stunning smile. Even wearing snow gear, Lacy could see that he was well-built.

"You want the usual?"

Derek nodded. "You got it, Sarah."

Lacy, realizing she was staring and whirled back around, took a frantic sip of her peppermint mocha. To her utter horror, the drink went down the wrong tube and she began coughing uncontrollably. Her eyes watered as she struggled to regain control of her breathing and she knew from the heat pouring off her cheeks that she must be blushing a furious red. Finally, wiping at her streaming eyes, she managed to clear her throat. She peeked over and saw Sarah and Derek making a valiant effort to hold back laughter.

"Just let it out," she groaned. "I know that looked ridiculous."

Gales of laughter exploded from them, so infectious and without malice that Lacy found herself joining in. The embarrassment that had clutched her began to fade a little. Still chuckling, Sarah handed Derek his coffee.

"Well, Ms. Preston, it seems you're met with

calamity wherever you go," Derek commented, his eyes twinkling. "It looks like you at least made it back to the inn last night safely."

Lacy wanted to be annoyed, she really did, but the laughter shining in his eyes made her smile in spite of herself. "Yes, Derek," she said, the tartness in her voice belied by her smile. "I may be a 'city girl' but I did manage the walk back to the inn, fraught with perils and danger as it was."

"So you two have met before?" Sarah asked, leaning against the counter and looking intrigued. "Do tell."

"We've definitely met," Derek replied, his eyes still on Lacy. "You could say we ran into each other last night."

"I wouldn't say *we* ran into each other," Lacy jumped in, eager to defend herself. "*Some* people think it's perfectly all right to race around the countryside in the dark, risking the safety of good, upstanding citizens who—"

"That's not the whole story," Derek interjected, his eyes dancing. "Like I said before, people from this town know not to wander around in the dark without a flashlight or a lantern!"

"Is anyone going to tell me what's going on?"

Sarah's ponytail swung as she looked from Derek to Lacy and then back again.

"I was taking one of my teams for a night trail run, Sarah, and we happened to be over by Nicholas Spielman's house. When we came over the hill behind his house, Lacy here was standing like a deer in the headlights. I only just managed to stop my team, and it definitely gave her quite the scare." He looked at Lacy apologetically now. "I really *am* sorry we scared you."

"Yes, so you mentioned last night," Lacy said with a touch of asperity as Sarah threw her head back and laughed uproariously. "All I'm saying is that you could be more careful."

"Derek is a sledding master in these parts," Sarah pointed out, wiping at her eyes. "That's why folks come from other towns to take lessons from him."

Lacy glanced at Derek, arrested again by his good looks and the tug she felt to learn more about him. Dogsledding didn't seem like a particularly important job, certainly not a 'real' job like hers, but she had to admit there was something intriguing about a man with such a unique career. Realizing she was staring at him again, she took a hasty sip of her mocha.

"That business is all thanks to your grandfather,

actually," Derek said to Lacy. "He helped me get the business loan I needed to open Winter Run Racing, and it changed my life. I wouldn't be where I am today without his help."

All the good humor drained out of Lacy at the mention of her grandfather again. Like Sarah, Derek had nothing but good things to say about the man. Nothing they said gelled with what she had believed all her life about her father and grandfather, and she knew if she thought about it too long she might disappear down a rabbit hole of confusion and emotion. Suddenly, the upheaval of the past week settled over her, and she began to feel a little queasy.

"Well, it was nice to meet you, Sarah, and thanks for the scone," Lacy said, taking her cardboard cup of coffee with her. "I'm sure I'll see both of you later."

She turned, hurrying to the door and pulling it open.

"Lacy," Derek called.

Just the sound of her name from his lips sent a twinge of something that felt suspiciously like butterflies erupting in her stomach, but she tried to ignore the feeling. Turning, she made eye contact with him and raised an eyebrow in question.

"If you want to come by my shop, I'll take you

out for a ride with the team. You know, since you rejected my offer last night."

Lacy's eyebrow arched even higher and a smile twitched at her lips. "Unlikely."

"Come on, if you give sledding a try, you'll fall in love with it, and maybe you'll forgive me for almost running you over."

Lacy couldn't hold back a real smile by then. "Like I said, unlikely," she replied with a smirk. "But thank you anyway."

With that, Lacy left the bakery, steadfastly refusing to acknowledge the butterflies that had moved from a twinge in her stomach to full-on flight.

CHAPTER SEVEN

Colette inhaled appreciatively, steam wafting into her face from the bubbling marinara sauce on the stove. Emma had taught Colette the recipe years ago —the same recipe that had been handed down from her own mother's mother. It was a favorite of hers, and she made a big batch of it at least once a month, parceling it out for use in various recipes. Tonight she would layer it in a homemade lasagna, another favorite recipe Emma had taught her a long time ago. The doorbell rang and Colette heard Emma shifting in the living room, struggling to rise from her armchair.

"I'll get it," Colette called. "You just stay comfortable."

Hurrying to the front door, Colette pulled it

open and waved Derek inside. "Derek! Emma will be so glad to see you."

"Is that my sweet boy at the door?" Emma called from the living room, making Colette and Derek both grin.

"Yes, ma'am," Derek replied, pulling off his snow boots before padding into the living room in his stocking feet to drop a kiss on Emma's fluffy white hair.

Emma reached out and grasped his hand, urging him to sit in the armchair beside hers. "Tell me how you've been doing. You know I don't get out much during the winter."

"Staying busy with work as always. I've got a new student, a little guy only seven years old. He's the cutest little kid, and the dogs all love him."

"He's lucky to have you, dear. I imagine he looks cute as a button on those baby sleds you use for the littler children."

"He really does." Derek laughed. "He's taken to sledding right away, and I think he'll be a fine dogsledder one day." He patted Emma's hand and nodded with his head to the knitting on her lap that she'd abandoned when he had come in. "What have you got there?"

"Oh, just another blanket. I'm knitting as many

as I can before Christmas. I'm sure you remember that the Holy Grace Church takes donations for the less fortunate, and I'd like to do my bit, little as it is."

"It's not 'little' at all," Colette chimed in, giving Emma a fond look. "She's already knitted ten blankets."

Derek gave a low whistle and Emma blushed a little. "You're a rare gem, Miss Emma. They're lucky to have folks like you."

"Oh, you." Emma fluttered her hands vaguely, waving away the compliments, but Colette could see from the happy color in her cheeks that Emma was pleased. "I spend so much time in this armchair anyway, I might as well do some good while I'm at it!" She picked up her knitting needles again. "You'll stay for dinner, won't you? Colette said she's making lasagna."

"Why do you think I stopped by for a visit around dinner time?" Derek asked, giving Emma a wink.

"You're a rogue and a scoundrel, my boy," Emma teased.

"Guilty." Derek's grin was entirely unrepentant as he rose to his feet. "That being said, I do try to earn my keep! Colette, let me help you finish putting dinner together."

Colette smiled her thanks and followed her cousin into the kitchen where her casserole dish was waiting for the lasagna to be assembled. She took up her station at the counter and laid down a layer of red sauce while Derek washed his hands at the sink, then laid down a layer of cooked lasagna noodles, followed by the ricotta and herb mixture.

"I have the fixings for a Caesar salad in the fridge," she said over her shoulder. "Would you mind throwing it together?"

"Not at all."

The two worked in companionable silence for a time, moving with ease through the kitchen. Colette finished with the lasagna and put it in the oven to heat through, then picked up a loaf of crusty Italian bread and began slicing it to make garlic bread. Derek, the salad finished, began chopping fresh garlic to make the garlic butter.

"How are things in town?" Colette asked, enjoying Derek's presence. The old house could get quiet at times, and she always enjoyed his company. "I haven't been out in a few days, especially since it was snowing all day yesterday."

"You know, I actually had an interesting run-in with a newcomer," Derek replied, and Colette glanced up at the studied nonchalance in his voice. He met her gaze, but she thought she caught the slightest hint of a flush on his temples.

"...and? Who is this newcomer?"

"Her name is Lacy Preston—she's Nicholas Spielman's granddaughter."

Colette dropped her knife and lifted a finger to her lips instantly, freezing and listening hard. When the steady click of Emma's knitting needles continued in the kitchen, she relaxed a bit and took a deep breath. Derek looked at her with a question in his eyes.

"Emma was in a relationship with Nicholas, remember?" Colette whispered.

Comprehension dawned in Derek's eyes. "Oh, that's right... I had forgotten. They were so old-fashioned about it all—like a courting couple back in the olden days."

Colette speared him with a look. "Which makes sense."

"Right, right, of course." He paused. "How has she been handling his death?"

"She hasn't really brought it up, which worries me. You remember this morning, when I told you she didn't quite seem like herself?"

Derek nodded.

"Well, now I'm wondering if she's been missing him."

Derek began spreading the garlic butter on the slices of bread. "It makes sense. It's only natural that she would be mourning him—in fact, I'm actually more worried about the fact that she hasn't shown *more* of a breakdown since he passed."

"We all handle grief in our own way. I just hope she knows she can talk to me when she's ready."

"Of course she knows that. You're more than the hired help, Col. You're like a daughter to her, you know that."

"I know. I'm just worried about her, that's all."

"Me too. Emma's a strong woman, though, and we shouldn't forget that."

"I know," Colette repeated, her voice thoughtful. "How's this Lacy woman handling things?"

Derek leaned against the counter and folded his arms. "She hasn't come right out and said anything, but I get the feeling she wasn't overly fond of Nicholas. Every time his name comes up she gets this... look on her face. It's kind of a closed off look, like she's shutting down inside, or—" He broke off, and Colette was now certain there was something going on with the woman that Derek wasn't mentioning, what with the way that same flush was spreading across his cheekbones again. "Anyway, I'm sensing there's a backstory there, but it's not like I know her well enough to ask her about it. I've only talked to her once or twice."

"Hmm..." Colette pulled the lasagna from the oven and put the garlic bread in, turning on the broiler to quickly toast the tops. "I wonder if it would be good for Emma and Lacy to meet. Maybe they could help comfort one another. Maybe Emma could help Lacy work through whatever history she had with Nicholas." Derek looked a bit doubtful, but Colette was already nodding to herself. "Lacy might make Emma feel as though a piece of Nicholas is still with her. After all, she's the granddaughter of the man Emma loved so much."

Derek put on some oven mitts and pulled the now-toasted garlic bread from the oven. "I'll give it some thought. Don't say anything to Emma yet, if you don't mind."

Colette hesitated, then nodded slowly. "I'll wait for you to give me the go-ahead."

* * *

Friday afternoon, tired of working on her laptop in her hotel room, Lacy made her way over to Sweet

Thing Bakery. It was quickly becoming one of her favorite spots in Snowy Pine Ridge, and she had certainly been working her way through the menu of treats at the bakery.

I'll need to ask around about a gym while I'm here, she thought, even though her trim figure hadn't changed in the slightest since her arrival. *Still, it doesn't hurt to stay in shape.*

She made a mental note to ask Sarah what the options were for a short-term gym in town as she made her way to Sweet Thing.

There was a line of customers waiting at the front counter when Lacy walked in, so she selected a booth and put down her laptop before shrugging out of her coat and getting settled in. On her laptop, she opened up the spreadsheet she'd been working on to keep track of the things she needed to buy for the house and then answered a couple of emails from the home inspectors she'd reached out to the day before. She got so lost in her work that she jumped a little when Sarah greeted her.

"How long have you been standing there?" Lacy gasped, one hand to her heart.

Sarah laughed, the infectious sound ringing through the bakery. "Just a couple of seconds. You didn't hear me the first time I asked how you're doing."

"Now that I'm past the mini-heart attack you just gave me, I'm doing just fine," Lacy replied with a laugh.

Sarah set down a plate with a flaky raspberry Danish on it. "Here, this is on the house," Sarah said, then sat down across from Lacy.

"Are you sure?" Lacy still couldn't get over how friendly the folks in Snowy Pine Ridge were. It was so different from the clipped and businesslike transactions she was used to in St. Louis. Back home, she'd visited the same Starbucks every day for years and she still didn't know the names of the workers there. "I really can pay for it."

"It's fine," Sarah said, waving Lacy's offer away. "You've already supported my business so much the past few days, I think you've earned it."

Lacy blushed a little, her mouth too full of the Danish's delicate sweetness to respond. Gulping down her bite and wiping her mouth with a napkin, she smiled sheepishly. "I think I've tried almost everything on your menu at this point."

"Hey, no complaints here! I've got bills to pay, sister."

"Great, so let's just say I'm doing my civic duty

and ignore the fact that I've developed a serious addiction to your pastries."

"Deal."

"Speaking of my pastry addiction, are there any gyms in town? I've got to find a way to work off all these sweets."

"Are you kidding me? You look amazing, Lacy!"

Lacy smiled, tucking her hair behind her ear. "You're sweet to say so. I just want to make sure I'm keeping up with my health for however long I'm here."

"We have an all-purpose gym, Fitness365, but I usually go to The Barre instead."

Lacy busted up laughing. "I'm sure a bar is a great place to work out," she teased.

Realizing what it had sounded like, Sarah threw her head back, her ponytail swinging as she laughed. "No, no, b-a-r-r-e. Like barre workouts? The kind ballerinas do?"

"I've heard of barre before," Lacy responded dryly.

"The Barre has yoga and Pilates as well."

"Perfect, I'll look them up. Thanks, Sarah!"

Sarah nodded at Lacy's laptop. "You were super focused when I came over here—what are you working on?"

Lacy was about to fob her off with some vague answer about work, but she suddenly realized how hungry she was for a friend. She hadn't talked to Madeline since she'd gotten to Snowy Pine Ridge, and she'd been spending long hours at the house. Sarah had been nothing but welcoming since her arrival, and she already really liked the baker. Just because she didn't plan on staying in town long didn't mean she couldn't make some friends while she was here, and she was desperate to unburden herself.

She leaned forward, tilting her laptop so Sarah could see the screen. "I'm trying to pick out some things for the house. Obviously, it's a Victorian home, so I'm trying to pick out colors and wallpapers and furniture that will be true to the time period." She clicked over to her web browser, showing Sarah some of the pictures she'd been looking at for inspiration. "What do you think?"

Sarah clapped her hands and began scrolling through the pictures, murmuring with approval as she looked at some of the items Lacy had been considering. They discussed some of the options, Sarah's enthusiasm spreading to Lacy and infusing her with an excitement she hadn't felt before.

"I'm loving this floral wallpaper," Sarah said,

pointing at the screen. "Especially if you paired it with a painted crown molding. That would look amazing in the sitting room."

Lacy felt her brow wrinkle. "You've been to the house?"

"Sure, most of the town has. Nicholas used to throw grand Christmas parties there every year." Sarah's eyes were wide as she drifted back in her thoughts, obviously remembering past parties. "Everyone would come, and the house looked so amazing with all the Christmas decorations. Nicholas would dress up as Santa every year, of course. He was our St. Nick."

Lacy listened silently, an emotional tug-of-war in her brain. Despite the bad blood between her and her grandfather, she couldn't help but be intrigued at the thought of the mansion in its heyday. She pictured the dusty rooms clean and warm, full of people laughing and talking, perhaps sipping wine and sampling Christmas treats, Christmas music swirling through the air... The thought hurt her heart a little—such a scene was so different from the lonely and quiet Christmases she and her mother had shared.

"Well, no matter what I pick," Lacy said, her

voice a bit abrupt, "I'm sure it will be an improvement. The place needs a *lot* of work."

"Do you know what you want to do with it yet?"

"Not yet, but I've got some time to figure it out. I have an inspector coming to see if it needs any work done on the plumbing or electrical or things like that. Until then, I can just focus on getting it cleaned up and seeing to some of the cosmetic repairs."

"Well, I think it's wonderful. You're going to breathe life into that beautiful home," Sarah said, beaming.

The lingering tension in Lacy's heart eased at Sarah's warmth and she smiled back, glad that she'd confided in Sarah. She was about to respond when a man stepped up to their table, a notepad in one hand and a pencil behind his ear. The two women looked up at him in question.

"I'm sorry to interrupt, ladies," the man said, "but I'm a columnist for the Evanston Gazette."

"Evanston is the next town over," Sarah said for Lacy's benefit.

The man nodded eagerly. "I couldn't help but overhear that you're planning to restore the Spielman mansion?"

Lacy nodded, still a bit bewildered.

"I'd love to write an article about it, if you're

open to it," the man continued, his words spilling out with enthusiastic haste. "What do you say?"

Sarah impulsively reached out and grabbed Lacy's hand, her face alight with excitement. "Wow," she breathed. "Look, word is already spreading about the work you're doing, Lacy!"

Lacy smiled back, considering the man's offer. If nothing else, it would drum up more excitement and awareness about her project, which might help when she tried to sell the house or flip it into some other investment. It was a smart business move, she decided.

She reached her hand out to shake the reporter's. "You've got a deal."

CHAPTER EIGHT

As soon as the doors of Mitchell Hardware opened at ten a.m. the next morning, Lacy was grabbing a cart and moving about the store with a purpose. She had spent the better part of the past week assessing, taking notes, and looking through ideas, and now she was itching to move forward in earnest. No more waffling, she had determined while lying awake in bed the previous night. It was time to actually dive into the project, which meant getting her hands dirty. She knew she didn't have loads of experience in that department, but the one thing she did know was that she, Lacy Preston, had never backed down from a challenge and she knew how to work hard.

Google will be my best friend during this whole thing, she thought as she threw some paint rollers and disposable paint trays into her cart. *And I'll be hiring contractors to do the skilled tasks. I can handle painting and cleaning, no problem.*

"Can I help you find anything?"

Lacy turned to see a man with curly brown hair and a close-trimmed beard standing a few feet from her. He stood only a few inches taller than her, but he was stocky and muscular. He wasn't wearing any name tag or uniform, and it suddenly occurred to her that some random man might have seen a lone woman in a hardware store and decided that she wouldn't know anything. Well, she didn't know anything, but *he* didn't need to know that, she decided, drawing herself up to look as tall as she could.

"Do you work here?" she asked, raising one eyebrow.

The man smiled, his brown eyes kind. "Clark Mitchell, at your service. And yes, you could say that."

"Mitchell... as in 'Mitchell Hardware.'" Lacy bit back a groan and hoped she wasn't blushing.

"That's me," he replied, cheerful as ever. "Anyway, like I said, happy to help with anything you need."

Lacy swallowed her pride, bitter as it was.

"Actually, I was wondering if you rent out floor sanders? And maybe shop vacuums that can deal with wet or dry messes?"

"Absolutely. We can take care of that at the register."

"Great. One less thing on my list."

"Need help with the rest of the list?"

"No, I'm good, thanks. A lot of this comes down to design and style choices, so it might take me a while. I'm headed to look at your wallpaper selection next."

"Okay, I'll get out of your hair then," Clark said with a grin. "Give me a holler if you need anything."

Lacy nodded her thanks and turned back to her cart. Over the next hour or so, she wandered the aisles, debating the various merits of paint colors and wallpaper selections and filling her cart with a mountain of cleaning supplies and basic tools. When she saw a small selection of coveralls usually used by mechanics, she went ahead and threw in the smallest pair she could find. Restoring the mansion would be a messy business, and she suddenly realized that not one piece of her stylish wardrobe was suitable. Finally, with great effort, she pushed her heavy cart up to the register, peeking around the corner of it to see Clark watching with an impressed look on his face.

"All right, let's see the damage," she joked, reaching into her purse to pull out her credit card. "And please don't forget the sander and the shop vac."

"You got it." Clark began scanning items and, in what Lacy decided was a very thoughtful gesture, packing them neatly into cardboard boxes to make the load easier to carry.

As she watched the total on the register climbing higher and higher, Lacy felt her chest tightening with something awfully close to panic, but she tamped it down with a herculean effort.

This is no different than when you invest in someone else's business venture, she scolded herself fiercely. *You've invested in yourself before too, so you've got this! Sure, you're about to take on work you've never done before, but you're Lacy Preston! You figure things out and you come out on top.*

The pep talk helped her to slow her breathing, but the grand total did still leave her wincing a bit. Investment or not, this money was coming out of her own account, and it was a doozy.

"Does the store have a delivery truck?" she asked,

handing over her credit card. "I need this delivered to the Spielman mansion."

"That's right, word has gotten around town that St. Nick's granddaughter was restoring it."

Lacy ignored the mention of her grandfather's nickname. "A delivery truck would be super helpful," she hinted.

Clark got the message. "The store does have one, but I can tell you right now that it won't make it up the hill to the mansion. Don't worry, though—my friend often helps out with deliveries in cases like this. Let me give him a call."

Relieved, Lacy thanked him. While she waited for Clark's friend to arrive, she began drafting a list on her phone of what tasks she would tackle first at the mansion. Having a plan of attack always helped her to feel more prepared, and she soon lost herself in the process of strategizing her efforts at the house. In what seemed like no time at all, Clark announced that his friend was here. With an effort, Lacy pulled her attention away from her phone just in time to see Derek walking through the sliding glass doors of Mitchell Hardware.

Lacy's jaw dropped. "There's no way you're a delivery man too," she said as he approached.

Derek grinned and Lacy was downright ashamed

of the way those pesky butterflies suddenly erupted in her stomach at the sight of it.

"I'm just used to navigating the snow, and my truck is the most reliable in town for getting through, so lots of folks call me for help with things like this."

"He's a regular knight in shining armor," Clark joked, clapping Derek on the shoulder, while Derek rolled his eyes.

"I'm going to take a wild leap and say that this mountain of supplies is for the mansion?"

Lacy nodded. "Yup, you can see how taking a box at a time on foot would take me a while."

The three of them began carrying boxes out to Derek's truck, and she instantly saw why he was called on to help people all the time. His pickup truck was massive, easily one of the biggest she'd ever seen. It practically exuded power and, though she didn't know much about trucks, she figured this one was an all-terrain off-roading type of rig. The huge wheels were covered in snow chains as well, which was an instant relief. The thought of sliding backward down a hill in a vehicle was *not* something she wanted to experience.

"This old boy is up to the task," Derek said, his voice close to her, and she jumped slightly, whirling to see him standing beside her.

"Excuse me?"

Derek slapped the side of his truck. "It looked like you were studying my truck, and I just wanted to reassure you that he can handle just about anything."

"The 'old boy' meaning your truck." Lacy bit back an awkward chuckle, but Derek laughed aloud.

"If you ever hear me refer to myself as an 'old boy' please, slap me on the spot and never speak to me again." Derek opened the passenger side door for her. "It's not a dogsled this time and I'm transporting your supplies anyway, so how about I give you a lift to the house?"

"Thanks, I appreciate it," she replied. Ignoring his proffered hand, Lacy grasped the door handle and heaved herself up into the cab of the truck, inordinately proud that she was able to do it without help.

Lacy had been used to taking care of herself for most of her life, and all of this small-town hospitality was still throwing her for a loop. It seemed that everywhere she turned, someone was offering to open a door or, in Sarah's case, offering her a free pastry. Derek made his way around the truck, climbing into the driver's seat with ease. The truck started up with a powerful growl when he turned the key in the ignition. Soon they were pulling out of the parking lot and making their way through the snowy streets.

"You know, you still haven't come by my shop for your complimentary dogsled ride," Derek pointed out as they drove. "My teams are starting to worry that you haven't forgiven them yet."

Lacy wasn't quite sure how to answer that, and she definitely wasn't sure how she felt about dogsledding in general. Best, she decided, to avoid the invitation in general.

"Your line of work is rather interesting. Not many people can say they work in the dogsledding industry." She glanced over at his profile. "What made you want to do it in the first place? How did you get started?"

"I think it all came together in one of life's interesting quirks of fate. An ex-champion dogsledder chose Snowy Pine Ridge as the place he wanted to settle down when his competitive career was over. He gave some of the people in town lessons, so dogsledding has pretty much always been a part of my life." Derek smiled at the memories. "When he moved away to retire closer to his family, I decided I didn't want dogsledding to leave with him, and I decided to carry on where he left off."

"It sounds like you've expanded on his original vision."

"A bit. I stay busy."

Derek pulled the truck to a stop in front of the mansion. Lacy blinked, shocked that the drive was already over. She had gotten so immersed in Derek's story that she hadn't noticed the truck easily taking on the hill leading to the mansion.

"Let me help you get unloaded," Derek offered, and Lacy was only too happy to accept.

They worked in companionable silence, forming an assembly line of sorts as Lacy climbed into the bed of the truck and handed him boxes, which he carried up the front steps and placed in the grand foyer. Once Derek had unloaded the industrial sander and shop vac for her, he pretended to tip his hat to her, which made her smile.

"Thanks for all your help. I really appreciate it."

"No problem." Derek pulled his phone from his coat pocket and glanced at the time, his eyes widening a little. "Annnd I'm late for a lesson. Sorry, I've got to run."

Lacy waved him away, thanking him one last time before climbing up the front porch steps. She could hear the rumble of the truck as it powered to life and began the journey back down the hill. As she wandered among the boxes in her foyer, looking at all her supplies, she couldn't help thinking about Derek.

A second pair of hands would be helpful right about now, she thought, then rolled her eyes at herself. As though she could hide her true feelings even from her own mind. *That's not why you wanted him to stick around, and you know it.*

"I don't know any such thing," she announced to the silent house around her, then rolled her eyes again. "And now I'm talking to no one. Come on, Lacy, get yourself together."

CHAPTER NINE

Colette always looked forward to Sunday evenings with Emma. In the summer they would sit out in the garden with some of Colette's homemade lemonade, always garnished with fresh mint, of course. In the winters, they would sit by the fire and drink hot chocolate. Even though they saw each other every day, there was something special about Sunday evenings together—Emma was usually mellow and contemplative, and it was often a time that she would tell Colette stories from her younger years. This particular evening, Colette had decided to spice things up and add raspberry liqueur. She swirled fresh whipped cream on each mug, then sprinkled dark chocolate shavings on top to finish off the entire rich confection.

"Emma," she called, "your hot chocolate is ready!"

She waited, but there was no response, no shuffling of Emma's footsteps down the hall. Puzzled, Colette poked her head into the living room. Emma's usual armchair was empty, her knitting half-finished and waiting in the basket beside her chair. Colette walked down the hall, checking the office and the guest bedroom, but there was no sign of Emma. Hearing a faint rustling sound, Colette tiptoed into Emma's bedroom, and the rustling sound got louder. It sounded as though it was coming from her closet.

When Colette peeked inside, she didn't see Emma right away. It wasn't until she looked closer that she realized Emma was bent over and rummaging in the back corner of her walk in closet. Her head and upper back were buried deep within the hanging clothes, leaving just her little rump poking out. Colette covered her mouth with her hand, stifling a laugh, although she couldn't help but smile so big her eyes crinkled at the corners. Not wanting to scare Emma or embarrass her, she stepped back into the bedroom and knocked on the bedroom door.

"Emma? Are you in there?"

The rustling sounds stopped. "Yes, dear, come in."

Colette stepped into the closet doorway again. Emma's fluffy hair was poking out in all directions, ruffled from her foraging and Colette had to bite back another smile even as a wave of love for the old woman filled her heart nearly to bursting.

"There you are," she said lightly. "Were you looking for something?"

Emma's face tightened a little and she wouldn't meet Colette's eye. "No, no..."

"Well, I have your hot chocolate ready. Why don't you come to the living room?"

Emma followed Colette down the hall and they were soon both settled in their armchairs, steaming mugs of hot chocolate in hand. Emma took a careful sip and then gave an approving nod, silently letting Colette know she approved of the new flavor. Colette took a sip of her own and sighed with pleasure.

Utter perfection, she thought, then took another long sip for good measure, licking the whipped cream off her lips.

Following Emma's lead, she picked up her own knitting. She was nowhere near as fast as Emma, who had taught her to knit many years before, but she could hold her own. Between the two of them, they would have a massive stack of blankets to donate to those in need. While they knitted in companionable silence, Colette kept one eye on Emma.

Her surrogate mother had been distracted and closed off of late, and she was certain that Emma was hiding something inside, something she wasn't yet ready to talk about. Her needles clicked along at an even more furious pace than usual, letting Colette know that Emma's thoughts were whirring along just as fast. Colette could always gauge Emma's mood by how she knitted.

Colette cleared her throat. "Nicholas Spielman's granddaughter has come to town," she said, careful to keep her voice casual. "Apparently he left her the house and she's going to fix it up."

The clacking of Emma's knitting needles stopped entirely, her hands suddenly still in her lap. Colette glanced at Emma's face and saw that Emma's eyes had grown watery and sad. The sight alone confirmed the suspicions Colette had been harboring all week—Emma was mourning for Nicholas and thoughts of him must have been at the forefront of her mind lately.

"I knew that he had a granddaughter," Emma

finally said, her voice quiet and a little raspy. She picked up her knitting needles again and held them, but seemed to have forgotten that she was supposed to be knitting. A moment later, her needles dropped back into her lap. "He always hoped she would get in touch, but she never did. I certainly never met her in all my time with Nicholas."

Colette took a sip from her mug, mulling Emma's words over, then finally spoke gently. "Well, according to Derek, it seems like Lacy—that's her name, by the way—doesn't have a very favorable opinion of Nicholas."

Emma's brow puckered with deep concentration.

"Emma, is everything all right?"

"It's just... hearing that Nicholas's granddaughter is in town... I think he left something for her. I'm sure of it, but I just can't seem to remember what it was..."

Seeing that Emma was becoming agitated, Colette reached out and patted Emma's hand and the older woman stilled beneath her touch.

"Emma, he *did* leave something to Lacy—the mansion."

Emma shook her head vehemently. "No, it was something else. He asked me to keep it for him, but I can't remember... .." Her fingers began plucking anxiously at the knitting on her lap.

Colette picked up Emma's mug and placed it gently in Emma's hands to give her something to hold on to. Emma took a mechanical sip and relaxed against the back of her armchair.

"Put it out of your mind for now," Colette said softly. "Let's just drink our hot chocolate for now. I'm sure it will come to you later."

Emma nodded, but Colette could tell her mind was miles away. Colette picked up her knitting and began working but, as she did, she kept one eye on Emma, worry mounting in her heart.

* * *

Lacy tucked the thick blanket around her toes more firmly, snuggling into the outdoor chair, and lifted her mug to her lips, taking a long drink of her spiced apple cider. After working on the mansion for three days straight, she was sore and stiff and more than ready to take a break. After coming back from tearing out old wallpaper and scrubbing away years of dust and neglect, Lacy had taken a long shower at the inn and pulled on some leggings and a hoodie. The covered back porch of the inn boasted a huge stone fireplace and the crackling fire within had tempted her back outdoors. With her blanket, her cider, and the fire, she was utterly cozy as she stared out at the snowy landscape.

Shifting to the side a little, she dug her cell phone out of her hoodie pocket and decided to give Madeline a call. She hadn't spoken to her friend since before she'd left for Snowy Pine Ridge and she knew Madeline was swamped at work, but she figured her friend would have time on a Sunday evening to relax. Taking another sip of her cider, Lacy found Madeline's name in her contacts and hit the call button. The phone rang against her ear only twice before Madeline picked up.

"Lacy! You're alive!"

Lacy smiled at Madeline's dramatic greeting. "Of course I'm alive, Mads. Phones work both ways you know—you could've called to check on me too."

Madeline ignored that comment. "I'm surprised you even have a cell signal out there in the boonies."

Lacy snorted. "Snowy Pine Ridge may be a small town but it's hardly the boonies. The hotel I'm staying in right now is like something straight out of a Christmas movie."

"Sounds magical. So I'm guessing that means things are working out beautifully, then?"

"Hardly. You would not believe the state of the mansion Nicholas left me."

"That bad?"

"It's got charm, for sure. I can tell beneath the grime and all the repairs it needs that it has good bones and lots of potential... .it's just going to take a lot more work to get there, and I've already been working myself to the bone."

"Hey, at least it's not an eyesore. If you're putting work into it, that means it's worth the effort."

"I think it will be." Lacy pursed her lips. "No, I *know* it will be. I've spent way too much on it already for it not to turn out well."

"Well, it's an investment for you. Speaking of, have you decided what to do with your investment yet?"

Lacy tapped one finger on the edge of her mug and blew out a frustrated sigh. "No. I still haven't been able to pin down what I want to do with it. Please, please, please tell me you have some ideas, because I'm lost over here."

"If this town is as adorable as you make it sound, then I bet it could work as a B&B. People go nuts for that kind of thing, especially in a dreamy little New Hampshire town."

"Maybe... the inn where I'm staying already has

something of a corner on that market. I don't know if it could compete."

"Well, what about turning it into office space? I know that sounds kind of crazy, but think about how many new startups want their businesses to run in a cool location—I mean, you're offering historic architecture, and you could subdivide it by floors or wings or something. Oh! Or what about turning it into a boutique?"

Lacy mulled these options over. "There's a lot of ideas there..."

"Well, if you don't like those ideas, you can just say so," Madeline huffed, and Lacy laughed.

"Relax, Mads. Your ideas are very helpful."

"Thank you." Madeline sniffed dramatically, then laughed and dropped her pretend angst. "Obviously, you know you could just sell it outright. Plenty of people are looking to move out of the big city and end up in a Hallmark card like this Snowy Mountain place."

"Snowy Pine Ridge," Lacy corrected automatically. "And you make a good point." She pulled the blanket around herself more closely. "You know, the craziest thing about being in this town is how much I keep hearing about my grandfather. Everywhere I turn it seems like someone new is coming out of the woodwork and they all have nothing but praise for him. It doesn't make any sense, Madeline. It certainly doesn't gel with what I knew about him my whole life."

"What do you think? Do you think he fooled them all?"

Lacy sighed. "I don't know. Mom never had anything good to say about him when she was alive, and she spent enough time around him to know. Before he and my father abandoned us, of course." She rubbed a hand against her forehead, not wanting to think about the confusing subject any longer.

Silence stretched across the line for a few moments and Madeline seemed to sense that Lacy's mood had darkened.

"We haven't discussed the most important thing yet," Madeline pointed out, breaking the quiet.

"And what's that?"

"Men! Have you met any hot lumberjacks?"

Lacy rolled her eyes, but she couldn't help but smile. "First of all, men are *not* the most important thing, and we both know that. Secondly... yes. But he's a dogsledder, not a lumberjack."

"Do tell," Madeline cooed, entirely ignoring Lacy's barb about men not being important. She and Lacy were both career women, but Lacy knew

Madeline was just trying to cheer her up and she appreciated the gesture. Besides, talking about handsome men made her feel like a teenager again, even though she'd had little to no time for dating back then either.

"Well, his name is Derek."

"And…"

"And that's all."

"Is he cute?"

Lacy laughed in spite of herself. "Very," she groaned, still smiling. "But it's not like it matters—I won't be here for long."

"Hey, just because you're not moving there doesn't mean you can't have some eye candy while you deal with the mansion."

"I'm not sure he would appreciate being called 'eye candy,'" Lacy pointed out with a laugh, "but he certainly does make this town more interesting…"

CHAPTER TEN

Lacy dipped her scrub brush into the bucket of cleaning solution and warm water before attacking the dirty grout once more. She had been on her hands and knees in the main floor bathroom of the mansion for a good two hours already that morning, scrubbing at the grout inch by hard-earned inch. The process was a painful and tedious one—her arms had been on fire since the first hour—but the original penny tile on the bathroom floors was too beautiful to rip out. And so, here she found herself, doing the unglamorous work of a scrub maid.

I need a break from ripping down wallpaper, she thought as she dipped the brush into the cleaning solution again. *I'm not sure this qualifies as a 'break' though...*

Another ten minutes passed in this way, but the end was in sight. By her estimate, she only had about a third of the floor left.

Which is still at least an hour of work, she realized with a groan.

The grout was so dirty that each spot of it required vigorous scrubbing multiple times before it came back to life. Tossing her scrub brush into the bucket of solution, she braced her hands against her aching lower back and stretched, wincing a little from her soreness.

I'm going to be cursing myself in the morning when I can't move my back.

Just as she was about to resign herself to her fate and pick up her brush once more, Lacy heard a faint whining sound. She froze, listening hard and, a few seconds later, the whimpering sound continued. It didn't sound human or like a fluke of the wind, but she couldn't tell what it was. Her heart hammering in her chest, she rose slowly to her feet and tiptoed out of the bathroom and down the hall, pausing every so often to listen for the sound again. Silently, she picked up a broom leaning against the wall, ready to use it as a weapon if need be.

Peeking into each room as she passed it, she

quickly became convinced that the sound was coming from outside the house. For a brief moment, she considered not investigating it, telling herself that she was acting like all the idiot people in horror movies that go hunting down strange noises instead of running for their lives.

But this is real life, she reminded herself sternly. *Besides, it's broad daylight. Stop being a chicken already!*

By now, Lacy had carefully pushed open the front door, thankful that she had oiled the hinges the week before so that now it glided open silently, and padded across the porch. Her back to the house, she peered around the corner of the house where the wraparound porch continued, and almost dropped to the ground in relief. The breath she'd been holding unconsciously now whooshed out of her as she sagged against the house for support. There, in a protected nook of the front porch, cowered a sweet little puppy.

"Oh, you poor baby," Lacy whispered, setting the broom aside and approaching it with caution so that it wouldn't flee. "How did you get here?"

The puppy whined some more. It was a husky with startlingly blue eyes that watched her with a deep sadness that nearly broke Lacy's heart. It let her approach, even pushing its head against her hand when she reached out to pet it. Lacy shivered, realizing she had forgotten her coat inside. Carefully, she reached down and scooped the puppy up, cuddling it close.

"You must be freezing," she murmured, already trying to figure out what to do with it. She wasn't set up to take care of a dog at the mansion.

And I don't even live here, she reminded herself.

She hurried back into the house, trying to think of what to do with the dog. It would need a good home. But where could she take it?

The answer hit her like a lightning bolt and she was surprised she hadn't thought of it right away. The perfect person to rescue this puppy was Derek.

"Come on, sweetheart," she said, shrugging into her coat and then cuddling the puppy close inside the coat. "Let's get you to Winter Run Racing. I have a feeling your new family is there."

* * *

Derek buffed the new varnish onto the wood of the sled he was repairing, losing himself in the familiar rhythm of the task. He didn't love every aspect of his job, but he always enjoyed maintaining his sleds and keeping them in tiptop condition. Dogsledding could be a rough sport, and it took quite a bit of work on the side to keep his stock of sleds in good working order. He had just begun singing along quietly with the classic rock station on the radio —"Open Arms" by Journey—when a movement outside the huge window in his shop caught his attention.

Dropping the rag with varnish onto his worktable, he peered through the window. Though it had only been a week, he would know that honey-brown hair anywhere. Lacy Preston was tromping through the snowy parking lot toward his shop, her head bent low against the wind. He looked a little closer, his brow furrowing. Her arms were wrapped around her middle, which looked oddly bulky and misshapen. Pulling open the shop door, he called to her and waved her in. Lacy barreled into the shop, her breath puffing out in vapors and her hair adorably windblown.

"I knew you'd come around," he announced, tossing her a grin. "I assume you're here for that free ride on one of my dogsleds?"

Lacy blinked, looking confused for a moment and then rolled her eyes. "Keep dreaming, pal."

Derek clutched at his chest, pretending to be wounded.

"Relax," Lacy laughed, "I'm actually here on important business."

"Oh?"

She opened her coat, revealing the source of the odd bulk around her middle: an adorable baby husky was tucked inside her coat. As the light of the shop hit its face, it blinked and yawned, causing them both to laugh. Lacy pulled it out, settling it into Derek's arms.

"I thought he—or she, I'm not sure which—might be yours?"

Derek shook his head. "This little one isn't mine." He quickly lifted it up and checked it out. "Where did you find this little lady?"

"She was curled up in a corner of my porch. You should have seen her." Lacy shook her head, her eyes becoming sad. "She was just whimpering and whining but she took to me right away. I don't know where she came from."

He sighed. "Unfortunately, this kind of thing happens all too often, especially with huskies."

Lacy leaned over and scratched behind the puppy's ears. "Why with huskies?"

"They can be a difficult breed for owners who

aren't prepared for them. Huskies are energetic and they need a lot of exercise and stimulation. New owners who aren't ready for that kind of commitment sometimes can't handle it and either put the dog up for adoption or just abandon them."

As the word 'abandon' left his lips, Derek noticed that Lacy visibly blanched and dropped her eyes, suddenly becoming closed off. Derek studied her face, noting how uncomfortable and pained she looked. There was a story there, something deep and painful, but he knew he had no right to ask.

"Do you think maybe she's just lost?" Lacy finally asked, breaking the charged silence. "Maybe her owners loved her and she just slipped out of the house by accident."

Derek's heart broke a little at the fragile hope in her voice. "No," he said gently. "I doubt it. She's not wearing a collar, and I can tell she's been out in the elements for at least a couple of days. I haven't seen any signs posted around town looking for a lost dog."

"Poor baby," Lacy murmured, hugging her arms closer to her chest. "She was probably freezing."

Derek finally cracked a smile at that. "Actually, that's one spot of good news—huskies are built for the cold. The temperature could've been even colder than this and she still would've been just fine."

Lacy gave him an incredulous look. "So does that mean I didn't need to stuff her into my coat?"

"Pretty much," Derek said with a laugh, "but it was still very sweet of you, and I'm sure she loved the human contact."

"So, what happens now? Do I take her to an animal shelter?"

Derek looked at Lacy, noting the sudden anxiety in her eyes and the question she clearly wanted to ask but wasn't asking. He had already made up his mind that he would take in the little dog, but he loved how much Lacy already cared about the fate of the puppy, even though she had just met it. For a woman who tried to remain tough and businesslike, this was a more tender side of Lacy that he hadn't seen before, and he liked it. Anyone who cared about animals the way he did was a good person in his book, and it told him a lot about the character of the woman standing in front of him.

"What happens now is that she'll stay with me," Derek said and Lacy gave an audible sigh of relief, the tension in her shoulders relaxing. "Huskies make excellent sledding dogs, but she's so cute I would've kept her either way." He winked at Lacy as he said the last bit, grinning when her cheeks pinked up adorably. There was something about breaking past her guard that intrigued him—he had a feeling that she was worth the work of getting to know. "Hey, I've got to pick up a few things for the puppy—some puppy chow and whatnot. Want to come?"

Lacy hesitated, biting her lip.

"Come on," he cajoled, "I'll bet you've been working on that house all day. Take a break."

"For all you know, I've been relaxing at The Snowy Pine."

"In your coveralls?"

Lacy looked down and cracked up, realizing the ridiculous figure she must be making in her work coveralls paired incongruously with her fancy peacoat. Derek held up the puppy, giving her some puppy dog eyes as well so they both looked like they were begging. Lacy threw up her hands, laughing even harder.

"All right, all right," she agreed. "You win."

"Don't sound so excited."

Lacy batted her eyelashes. "Whatever do you mean? I'm over the moon to run errands."

Derek's stomach flipped a little, but he covered his reaction quickly by teasing her. "Like it or not, we now have shared custody of a dog, and I'll thank you to do your part with some grace. After all, she's going to live with yours truly, so this is really the least you can do, you grump."

"A grump? Me?" Lacy put her hand to her chest, pretending to be affronted.

"Yes, you," he teased. "Come on, slowpoke, let's get this little lady the supplies she needs."

CHAPTER ELEVEN

Once Lacy had managed to climb into Derek's truck and get situated, she opened her arms for the puppy. Derek lifted it up to her and then closed the door, hurrying around the truck and hopping into his seat with an ease that Lacy envied. The puppy, tongue out as she surveyed her new surroundings with excitement, began wiggling in Lacy's lap as the truck roared to life. She pushed her wet nose against the window, her tail thumping against Lacy's legs as she stared at the moving scenery, only to turn around on Lacy's lap a moment later and sniff at Lacy's clothes or give her a sloppy kiss on the cheek. Lacy laughed, wiping her cheek off and Derek glanced over with a grin.

"She's a bundle of energy," he commented, "but that's a good sign."

"Yeah?"

"Yup. The energetic pups usually end up making the best sled dogs. With the proper training, this little lady will learn how to channel all that energy into sledding."

The puppy stared up into Lacy's eyes, its own wide and adoring, and Lacy's heart melted even more than it already had since she found it. It gave a soft *woof*, nudging her hand with its little nose until, laughing, she gave in and petted it. The puppy wiggled with excitement as Lacy scratched between her ears and under her chin.

"You remind me of Chicken," Lacy cooed at the puppy, surprising a laugh out of Derek.

"She reminds you of a *chicken*? In what world does a Husky remind you of a chicken?"

"Chicken with a capital C," Lacy clarified.

"That answers absolutely none of my questions— if anything, I have several more now."

Lacy couldn't stop grinning at Derek's utterly mystified expression. "Growing up I had a dog named Chicken. She was a Boxer and obviously she looked nothing like a chicken, but I was a toddler when we got her. According to my mother, I used to call every animal I saw a chicken, so..."

"So when you met your new puppy for the first time, naturally you shouted 'Chicken!'" Derek finished for her, a delighted smile growing on his face.

"Bingo."

"Hey, Lacy?"

Lacy scratched the back of the puppy's neck. "Hmm?"

"I feel that it's my civic duty to tell you that 'Chicken' is the worst name I've ever heard for a dog."

Lacy gave a mock-outraged gasp, drawing herself up in her seat and pinning him with a glare. "I'll have you know that Chicken *loved* her name, thank you very much."

"I think she just loved *you*."

Lacy pursed her lips, then laughed. "Okay, maybe so. Honestly, from the moment I met her, she and I became inseparable. We did everything together, and she would wait by the window for me to get off the school bus every day for years."

Derek's eyes were soft when he glanced over at her. "She sounds really special. A good dog makes its home in your heart and stays there long after they're gone."

Lacy nodded, her throat suddenly too tight to speak. She swallowed and blinked back a tear, surprised that thinking about her childhood dog could still make her emotional. Absentmindedly, she ran her fingers through the puppy's thick fur, glad that Derek had to watch the road and couldn't see her face clearly. She was never too comfortable with people seeing her emotions, especially when she was on the brink of tears.

"Do you have any pets now?" Derek asked, his voice light, and Lacy knew he was trying to lead her to happier thoughts.

"No," she admitted. "I always wanted to get another dog, but I got so busy with school and then with work. I work long hours, and it just didn't seem fair to keep a dog cooped up at home without me all day long."

"Makes sense."

Lacy looked out the window, her chest tightening now. In the space of a few moments, she had remembered the loss of her childhood puppy and realized how lonely her life was. Having a pet brought a special kind of comfort, and it was a comfort she hadn't known in years. Sure, with the hours she pulled in every week for her career, she was ill-suited to being a dog owner, but the hole in her life was one she'd always regretted, especially now that she had time to really consider it. She loved her work, but time and again she'd had to sacrifice for it in sometimes unexpected ways, including the simple and beautiful pleasure of having a dog. Feeling Derek's eyes on her, she glanced over at him and he quickly looked back at the road, but not before she'd seen the softness in his gaze, as though he could sense what she was thinking and feeling.

"What about a cat?"

Lacy blinked, the unexpected question throwing her for a loop. "What about cats?"

"You know, as a pet. They do pretty well with plenty of alone time during the day. Have you ever thought about getting a cat?"

The idea was so ludicrous that Lacy couldn't hold back a sudden peal of laughter. "Emphatically *no.*"

"My bad, my bad," Derek backpedaled, laughing too. "I didn't realize you were so passionately anti-cat."

"Anyone who knows me, knows that cats and I don't get along."

"Are you saying I don't know you?" Derek demanded, pretending to be offended.

"One hundred percent yes. We only met a few days ago."

"I'm crushed. After all we've been through!" Derek shook his head, raising an eyebrow and tossing a look her way. "Not only have we met several times, I've even saved your life. That kind of experience bonds people for life."

"Saved my life?" By now, Lacy's shoulders were shaking with laughter. "You mean, endangered it! You almost ran me over."

"'Almost' being the key word," he reminded her with a sniff. "Notice that I did not, in fact, actually run you over. Ipso facto, I saved your life."

Lacy threw her hands up in surrender. "How can I argue with that logic?"

"You can't." Derek shot her a satisfied smirk. "So, what's the deal with you and cats?"

"Well, for starters, cats don't listen to you. They just do whatever they please, and it drives me nuts. Seriously, I'm a dog person through and through."

"Lacy Preston, you are truly a woman after my own heart."

Lacy's breath hitched a little at his words, but she covered it by quickly petting the puppy again so she could regain her composure. Her cheeks began heating with what must surely be a blush, and she mentally ordered herself to get herself together and stop reacting to the tiniest compliment like a schoolgirl with a crush. To her relief, Derek didn't seem to notice her reaction.

"Of course," Derek continued. "Dogs do come with their own set of challenges."

"I bet you've got some good stories."

"Oh, I do, believe me. Do you want to hear about the time when a dog I was training chewed on each and every one of my shoes in one night and I had to wear mangled shoes until I could buy new ones? Or, how about the time I went to get the newspaper wearing only a towel when one of my dogs grabbed the towel to play? That one ends with me, standing on my porch in nothing but my birthday suit just as my elderly neighbor got home from early morning Mass."

By now, Lacy was chortling, her sides beginning to hurt from so much laughter. "No way," she gasped between gales of hilarity, her eyes streaming. "That did not happen!"

"Oh, believe me," Derek said grimly, though his eyes twinkled, "that story is very, very true. My neighbor is probably scarred for life, poor woman."

Lacy considered his muscular frame. "I doubt it —you probably gave her the thrill of a lifetime."

As soon as the words slipped out of her mouth, Lacy wanted to reel them back in and never, ever let them see the light of day. Her eyes widened with mortification as she realized what she had just said, unthinking, and she clapped a hand over her mouth.

"Lacy Preston, for shame," Derek pretended to scold, but she could see he was fighting a losing battle with the smile that was threatening to break free.

To her relief, they pulled into the parking lot of the town's pet supply store just then, and Lacy pretended to be wrapped up in unbuckling her seat belt and opening the car door. Not waiting for Derek's help, she jumped down from the truck's step, still holding the puppy, and waited for Derek to join her. They walked through the sliding glass doors together and that particular odor of pet food and animals that pervades every pet store greeted them. An eccentric-looking middle-aged woman wearing chunky beads and thick teal-framed glasses hurried up to them. She smiled wide, revealing a small smear of her magenta lipstick on one of her teeth.

"Well, look at this cute little puppy," the woman

gushed, her hands to her chest. "Just who is this little munchkin, Derek?"

"Penelope, this is Lacy Preston, she's visiting," Derek said, introducing the two women. "Lacy, this is Penelope Archer. She owns the store."

"Nice to meet you," Lacy said. "As for this little lady's name... we haven't actually picked one out yet."

"So the two of you are sharing this puppy?" Penelope looked between them, looking intrigued and ready for some juicy gossip.

Lacy felt her neck heating up, but Derek stepped in and handled the situation with an ease Lacy couldn't help but admire.

"No, Lacy found this sweet little gal abandoned and brought her to me, since you know I take in plenty of strays and train them to be sled dogs. She was just kind enough to come with me to grab some supplies."

Penelope looked disappointed for a moment, but she quickly brightened and cooed at the puppy. "Then let's get this adorable little thing all the goodies she needs."

"Sounds good, Penelope. I'm going to need a bag of puppy chow and a collar. Oh, and we'd better throw in some disposable mats, since I don't know if she's house trained yet."

The three walked through the store as Penelope filled a cart for them. To her surprise, Lacy actually liked the odd woman. Normally, she had little patience for personalities like Penelope's, but with Derek's calming presence behind her, she found that she didn't mind at all. Almost before she knew it, Penelope was ringing up the total and swiping Derek's card. Lacy offered to split the cost, but Derek waved her offer away with a sincere thanks.

"Seriously, don't worry about it. This puppy will join my sledding teams, which means I can write these supplies off on my taxes. We're good."

"If you're sure..."

"I'm sure."

Soon, Derek was loading the supplies into the back of the truck and helping her climb back up into the passenger seat. Lacy buckled up, settling the puppy onto her lap. Derek started up the engine and pulled out of the parking lot, heading back toward Lacy's house. She paused inwardly, realizing that she had thought about the mansion as hers, rather than her grandfather's, for the first time since she had learned of her inheritance. Not sure how she felt about that revelation, she turned to Derek.

"Do you know everyone in this town? It seems like everywhere we go, people know you by name."

"It's a small town," he pointed out.

"So if we walked into the grocery store right now, you'd know every person we came across there?" Lacy raised a skeptical eyebrow.

"Okay, not everyone, but definitely a lot. Besides being a small town, I host a lot of events through my business, so I meet a lot of folks. It's nice, most of the time, except when you have to run a quick errand and you're not looking your best."

Lacy folded her lips, making a physical effort not to joke about his towel mishap again. As if reading her mind, Derek shot a look at Lacy, raising a hand. "Don't you dare," he warned, his eyes already dancing with mischief.

"Don't I dare, what?" Lacy schooled her features into an innocent expression, inwardly surprised that she and Derek could already joke about her inappropriate reaction to the same story earlier.

"Yeah, yeah, play dumb," Derek teased, "but I know you were thinking it."

"You can't read my mind, Derek Morse, so don't even try."

"Is it a dark and twisted maze?"

Lacy rolled her eyes and pulled a face. He didn't

need to know about her painful past. "More like an endlessly running to-do list. Or maybe a massive spreadsheet. I swear I spend most of my working life staring at figures on a spreadsheet."

Derek pretended to shudder. "Reason number one thousand seventy-six that I'm glad I spend most of my working days outdoors and with dogs. Math and me are not friends."

"I've seen enough to know that your business is doing just fine, so I'm willing to bet you're better at math than you say."

"Accountants and bookkeepers are a wonderful help in that department," he said fervently, pulling the truck to a stop outside the mansion. "Okay, here we are. I hope me and this little puppy didn't take too much time out of your day."

Lacy unbuckled her seat belt, suddenly dreading going back to work on the house. She'd been having so much fun with Derek that the time had flown by, and for a split-second she considered fabricating an excuse to keep spending time with him. Horrified, she firmly shut that notion down and reminded herself that she was in Snowy Pine Ridge for one reason only—to fix up the mansion and figure out what to do with it. This trip was about business, nothing more.

Like a familiar piece of armor, she felt herself slipping back into her usual "work" mode—focused with laser-like precision on her goals and ready to work as hard as it took to get there. She knew this mentality like the back of her hand, but she found that it irked her a bit in that moment. Usually her work mode made her feel powerful and unstoppable, but today it felt a bit like an unwelcome restraint, even if it was necessary. Derek, she couldn't help but notice, was also looking a bit regretful as he took the dog.

"Thanks for your help with her," Lacy said, opening the door and jumping down. "I appreciate it."

"No worries. Always room for another dog at Winter Run Racing." He looked for a moment like he wanted to say more, his eyes searching hers, but then he shut his mouth and waved. "Okay, I'll get out of your hair. See you around."

Lacy closed the door and waved, stepping back as his truck tires sent up a soft spray of powdery snow. A moment later, he was gone, the truck disappearing back down the hill.

CHAPTER TWELVE

Lacy had spent Tuesday combing over the mansion with the inspector she'd hired, making note of the issues he had pointed out to her. To her surprise (and relief) the foundation of the house was fine, as was most of the wiring, but he did point out that some of the pipes would need to be replaced by a plumber and, of course, that the broken windows needed to be repaired. Though she had known that the house was potentially hiding some expensive repairs, she still winced inwardly as she began totaling up the potential cost of the repairs in her head.

Wednesday morning, as she began ripping out the already-peeling wallpaper in one of the second floor bedrooms, Lacy considered her next steps.

I've already poured so much work into this place,

she thought, tugging at a particularly stubborn strip of wallpaper. *These new repairs will cost a lot, but that's part of what comes with an investment. If you do things right, it just increases the value of the investment. This will be worth it in the end.* Lacy finally managed to peel the stubborn paper off the wall. *Or, at least, I hope so.*

She had just settled into a good rhythm, peeling the strips of paper off the walls and throwing them into the waiting trash bag, when she heard the sound of racing steps on the first floor, quickly followed by a resounding crash. Heart in her throat, Lacy sprinted down the stairs and raced toward the back door.

She sagged against the door frame in the back mudroom, heart racing, when she saw the puppy she'd rescued trotting in circles in the small room. A can of gorgeous midnight blue paint was now tipped over, the paint pooled and splattered across the worn and cracked linoleum floor. When the puppy saw Lacy, she raced over to her, barking and jumping up on Lacy's legs.

Not even two seconds later, Derek charged down the hallway from the front door.

"Lacy," he gasped, looking around at the mess in horror and raking a hand through his already windblown auburn hair so that it stuck out at crazy angles. "I'm so sorry! Let me help you clean this up." He turned from side to side, already looking for cleaning supplies. "I'm so sorry about the floor. I'll pay to have it repaired—-"

Lacy cut him off, laughing a little. "Whoa, whoa, slow down and take a breath."

Derek froze, blinking a little and looking stunned. "We just ruined your floor. How are you so calm right now?"

"Have you seen this place? It needs a ton of work."

"And I just added to it."

Lacy shrugged. "Not really. That linoleum floor is an eyesore, and ripping it up was on my to-do list."

"You're not just saying that?"

"Scout's honor," Lacy promised.

Derek blew out a relieved sigh, then brightened. "So, in a way, we did you a favor—spilling paint on this floor ensures that you'll definitely rip it out even if you're sick of working on this house. Can I get a word of thanks?"

Lacy put her hands on her hips and stared him down, narrowing her eyes. "Mr. Morse, I can see that I should've made you sweat a little more. I could've gotten you to do the work for me since you were so worried just a second ago."

"But you were sweet and laid my fears to rest," he replied, his usual cheerful manner fully intact once more. "A good businesswoman knows never to show all her cards at once, you know. Hey, free business tip! Now it looks like I've done you *two* favors today."

Lacy reached out and gave him a joke punch in the arm. "Very funny. Keep it up and see what happens."

He raised an eyebrow and shot her a look that sent butterflies erupting in her stomach. "What would happen?"

She hoped fervently that she wasn't blushing. She lifted her chin and folded her arms, trying to look stern. "I'd enlist you to do all the worst chores around this house so I wouldn't have to."

Just then the puppy, tired of being ignored, began threading its way back and forth between Lacy's and Derek's legs, clearly wanting some attention. Lacy laughed and crouched to give the puppy some good scratches.

"I'm happy to help anytime, in all seriousness."

Lacy looked up at him and smiled. "I might take you up on that." A thought suddenly occurred to her. "Wait a minute, why are you and the dog here this morning anyway?"

Derek cleared his throat, suddenly looking a little awkward. "The dog wanted to see you," he said, flushing a little and clearing his throat again. "I mean, I thought you'd want to see how the dog was doing. And to help me think of a name, since I haven't been able to think of one yet."

It took all of Lacy's willpower to hold back a teasing grin at his obvious discomfort. His pretext for visiting was fairly flimsy, sounding more like a fabrication than a necessary reason for a visit, but she wasn't complaining. She had found since arriving in Snowy Pine Ridge that she gladly welcomed any chance to see Derek, even if she didn't like to admit it to herself.

Under Lacy's knowing gaze, redness crept up Derek's neck and he stuffed his hands into his pockets as though he didn't know quite what to do with them. This kind of awkwardness was an entirely new side of the usually confident man, and she wondered just what had him so flustered that day.

"I see," Lacy murmured.

Derek chewed the inside of his cheek for a moment and then his expression cleared, as though he had come to an inward decision. "Actually, that's not the only reason I came over today."

Lacy stood back up, leaning against the door frame and waiting for him to continue, trying to ignore the fact that her heart had begun beating faster.

"I think we both know that it's pretty clear you're falling in love," he began, and Lacy almost blanched on the spot at his words. "With the puppy," he hastened to clarify, his cheeks reddening even more. "And since this little gal is a sled dog—or, at least, she will be one day—I think it's about time you finally take me up on that offer for a free ride."

Lacy hesitated for a moment, considering his offer. Her senses had frozen for a moment when he'd said she was falling in love, and for a split second she had thought he meant with *him*.

The thought had sent her into a tailspin, but she had also been surprised to feel a twinge of disappointment when he'd explained what he'd really meant. That split second of disappointment left her feeling more than a little flustered and frustrated with herself. Derek shuffled a little, and she realized he was still waiting for an answer. To her surprise, she realized that she wanted nothing more than an excuse to spend more time with him.

"Sure, why not?" She tucked her hair behind her ear, hoping she sounded casual and nonchalant, but knowing by the way her voice cracked a little at the end that she'd probably failed entirely.

Derek grinned and relief filled his eyes. "See, I knew you'd come around. No one can say no to dogsledding."

Lacy rolled her eyes even as she smiled. "Especially when they get invited so persistently."

"Just don't make me have to work so persistently to nail down a time for this free ride, okay?"

"How about tomorrow?"

"Works for me."

Lacy realized that she and Derek had stepped closer during the course of their conversation and now their gazes had caught and held. Her heart began beating harder once again, and she hoped fervently that he couldn't tell that she was having trouble breathing. *This is totally unlike me*, she thought. She had dated a reasonable amount in her life, but she'd never experienced this smitten sense of infatuation before.

Derek took a step back, preparing to leave, and then tripped on a broom she'd left lying on the floor from a previous day's work because he hadn't broken their eye contact. He staggered, his arms windmilling until he regained his balance. Lacy covered her mouth with her hands, fighting valiantly to stifle the laughter that threatened to burst out of her at the sight.

It was oddly comforting, she realized, to see Derek looking a little unsure of himself. He was always so confident and unflustered, but asking her out had seemed to bring out his awkward side. Her relief wasn't malicious. Rather, it was just nice to know that she wasn't alone in feeling a little infatuated and off-kilter.

"Well, now that I've thoroughly embarrassed myself, I'm gonna get out of here," Derek said, straightening up and chuckling. "It's okay, you can laugh."

"Me? Laugh? I would never."

"I applaud your valiant efforts," he said dryly, though his eyes twinkled. He turned to go.

"Aren't you forgetting something?"

Derek looked back, his expression confused. Lacy nodded to the puppy, and he reddened again. He whistled and the puppy trotted over to him. Derek bent down and scooped her up. "Okay, now I'm really, truly going to head out."

He was almost to the back door when Lacy thought of something.

"Missy," she called.

Derek turned back, looking confused once more.

"For the puppy's name. I think we should name her Missy."

"Missy?"

Lacy felt herself starting to blush, but she went ahead and said it anyway. "Because she's like a little Christmas miracle. It's short for Mistletoe."

Derek grinned and bent his head to drop a little kiss on the puppy's head. "Well, look at that. Her name is working already."

CHAPTER THIRTEEN

Derek glanced at the clock on the back wall for what was probably the hundredth time in the last twenty minutes. Only about a minute had elapsed since his last check, and he shook his head.

Come on, Derek, get it together. It's not even a date, technically, and it's not like she's even sticking around. She's just in town to restore the mansion. She's not here to stay. Chill out.

His little pep talk did next to nothing to calm the slight bout of nerves simmering just below the surface, nor did it tone down the excitement that overrode the nerves. If there was one thing he was absolutely confident in, it was his life's work.

He hoped Lacy, who had been more than a little standoffish about going dogsledding, would finally see just how magical the experience really could be. And "magical" really was the right word for it, cheesy as it sounded.

Working with a steadiness that belied those simmering nerves, he tightened a bolt that was just beginning to loosen on the sled he'd picked for Lacy's ride. The bolt was still well within safety limits, but he wasn't about to take any chances—he was doing anything and everything he could do on his end to ensure a smooth ride.

Glancing at the clock again and then rolling his eyes at himself for doing it, he gave the sled one last safety check. Satisfied that everything was in order, he mentally checked through the list of dogs he'd decided to use for his team that day.

The clock he was now beginning to despise told him that it was only one minute before nine in the morning, the time they'd decided to meet up. He'd texted Lacy the night before, asking what time he should pick her up from The Snowy Pine, but Lacy had stubbornly insisted that she would walk from the inn. When he'd pointed out that his mother had raised him to be a gentleman, she had lobbed back the shot that she was an independent woman who knew how to take care of herself.

Well, his mother had raised him to be a

gentleman all right, but she also hadn't raised a fool. Seeing that the argument was a futile one, he had relented. A knock on his shop door pulled him from his thoughts and he turned just in time to see Lacy poking her head into the shop.

"Come on in," he called and grinned as he took in the sight of her rosy cheeks, red from the cold air. "Wishing you'd taken me up on my offer to give you a ride?"

Lacy smirked, stepping fully into the shop. "Hardly. Derek, have you ever read *Pride and Prejudice*?"

Derek's brow furrowed, thrown for a loop by her non-sequitur. "I've seen the movie. Does that count?"

"Because I'm feeling generous, I'll say it does." Lacy arched an eyebrow at him, a teasing smile curling her lips. "Remember when Elizabeth walks three miles to Netherfield? All Darcy notices is that her eyes are brightened by the exercise. My walk this morning was less than ten minutes, but I think I should still get the same kind of response."

Derek was tempted, oh so tempted, to point out that she had just compared them to Darcy and Elizabeth—and even *he* knew that they were one of literature's major love stories—but he held his tongue. Instead, he decided to play along.

"Well, Miss Preston, allow me to tell you that your, uh... cheeks and nose have been brightened by the exercise..." He followed this up with a flourishing bow.

Lacy glared at him, her gloved hands on her hips. "My *cheeks?* My *nose?*" She rolled her eyes but couldn't suppress a grin. "You're hopeless. All right, let's get this over with."

"'Get this over with'? Lacy, I'm hurt." He surveyed her outfit, noting that even though she looked elegant and lovely in her expensive-looking cashmere sweater and skinny jeans tucked into knee-high leather boots, she was hardly dressed for dogsledding. "On a more serious note, we're going to have to find you some winter gear."

Lacy looked down. "I put on my most practical outfit—aside from my coveralls, that is."

"You look really nice," he promised, "but the sled kicks back a lot of snow, and it gets really cold out there."

"Well, I don't really have anything else..."

"Not to worry, I have snowsuits that folks can rent out when they come for lessons or pay for rides. Come on, let's go find one that will fit you."

Lacy hesitated. "So a lot of other people will have worn whichever snowsuit you give me?"

"I did fail to mention that I get the snowsuits washed. Does that ease your fears?"

"Very much." Lacy gave a relieved sigh. "Okay, take me to your most fashionable snowsuit."

Derek knew he had at least a few snowsuits in his rental section that would fit her, but he wasn't about to tell her that. Instead, he told her to wait there and went to pick out the most garish suit he had in her size—a relic from the eighties most likely, judging from the brazenly neon greens and pinks it sported. He returned, carrying it like a prized trophy.

"Would this suit her highness? I assure you, Miss Preston, this is the height of winter fashion."

Lacy's jaw dropped at the sight of the hideous suit, then looked over at him. Seeming to read the devilish gleam in his eye, she drew herself up and smirked, silently meeting his challenge.

"Luckily for you, I make everything look good," she said in a high-and-mighty tone, reaching out her hand for the suit.

Derek handed it over and Lacy began tugging the suit on, wobbling as she almost lost her balance. Derek shot forward and offered his arm so that she could steady herself, and she smiled by way of thanks. He tried not to notice how close they were to each other now, reminding himself that they would be even closer on the sled, but he was all-too-aware of the electricity shooting through his arm from her touch. Soon, she was suited up, looking both silly and utterly adorable in the neon snowsuit.

"Okay, safety first," he said, stepping into his business mode for a moment. "To have a truly enjoyable ride, we have to go over some procedures first. Here's what you can expect."

Over the next five minutes, he showed Lacy the sled, how it worked, and how to stay safe while riding. She listened with concentration, nodding and asking intelligent questions as he showed her the ropes of dogsledding. After that, it was only a matter of pulling the sled out the back of the shop to the snowy backyard that fed up into the trails, where she waited while he harnessed up his best team. In no time at all, Lacy was stepping up onto the sled and he stepped up behind her, putting his arms around her. He caught a whiff of her shampoo, or perhaps a perfume, as he boarded the sled, and the clean, flowery scent made his knees a little weak for a moment.

You're a professional. Get it together, he

reminded himself, for what felt like the millionth time.

"Hold on tight, spider-monkey," he joked.

Lacy twisted around in his arms to look up at him with an expression of disbelief. "Did you just quote *Twilight* at me?"

Derek threw her a grin. "Just thought I would show you how well-read I am." She tilted her head to the side, her eyes challenging him. "Okay, fine, I only saw the movie on that one too, and it was under duress."

"It's okay," Lacy cooed, batting her eyelashes. "You can admit you love vampire movies for teens. I think it's just the sweetest!"

Derek groaned. "I set myself up for that, didn't I?"

"You sure did," she agreed as she turned and held onto the handles. "Okay, Derek, mush!"

"Yes, ma'am," he replied meekly.

With that, he gave the dogs their cue to go, and they sprang forward. Immediately, he was back in his element. With deft ease, he guided the dogs up an easy trail that would lead to a ridge on the mountain with an excellent view of the town below. Lacy yelped a little as the sled shot forward even though the pace was light, gripping the handles even harder and standing stiff as a board. He doubted she was even taking in the pine trees sliding past or the sun making the fresh snow sparkle.

"Are you all right?" he asked, not even having to raise his voice much, since he'd kept his team to a leisurely pace.

"Well, the only winter activity on my bucket list this year was to go ice skating. You know, something normal."

He appreciated that, even though she was clearly nervous now that the sled was in motion, she was still trying to keep a sense of humor about it. "Dogsledding is normal," he insisted. "Well, at least it is in this town."

Lacy's ramrod straight posture and death grip on the handles hadn't relaxed an inch, so he called to his team to stop. The sled slid to a gentle halt and he looked down at her, tugging her to turn gently so he could make eye contact.

"Are you really okay? If this is too much for you, we can turn around."

Lacy hesitated, clearly unsure. "No," she finally said, "I can do this."

A strange sense of pride spread through Derek at her words. Even though dogsledding was as natural to him as breathing, he knew that for others it could be nerve-wracking, especially since they weren't in control of the sled. And, if there was anything he knew for sure about Lacy, it was that she liked to be in control. That suddenly gave him an idea.

"You work in investments, right?"

Lacy blinked, a little surprised by his seemingly random question, but nodded.

"Well, if I were needing financial advice, I would trust you as the expert. When it comes to dogsledding, that's where you can trust me." He searched her eyes, seeing understanding dawn in them. "I promise, I know what I'm doing."

She pulled in a deep breath and, to his surprise, she nodded. "Okay, that makes sense," she said simply. "I trust you."

She turned back around to face the front, so she didn't see how much her statement affected him. Taking a moment to gather himself, he then placed his arms back around her, noting that she had already relaxed a good deal. With another call, his team moved forward once again. He kept them at a slow pace at first, but, seeing that she was handling things much better, he allowed them to go a little faster. Soon, they were gliding along the trail with practiced ease, climbing up the incline steadily and taking the turns in the trail gracefully.

"It's so beautiful!" Lacy's voice floated back to him, laden with awe as her head swiveled side to side as they rode. "I've never seen anything like it."

"It never ceases to amaze me," he replied, although the scenery, which usually held his full attention, was actually secondary for him on this particular ride. If he was being honest with himself, he was more than a little distracted by the feel of her leaning against him and that tantalizing perfume that flew back to him every now and again.

A while later, the trail turned and they climbed the last incline before they reached the landing that overlooked Snowy Pine Ridge. He called to his team, giving the command to stop, and they slowed to a halt. Derek stepped off the sled, helping Lacy down and leading her to look out over the scenery. The town spread below them, laid out in its charming streets and surrounded by sloping hills laden with pine trees. In every direction, the gorgeous New Hampshire landscape spread around them.

Lacy stood silently, taking it in, and Derek noticed that she was blinking back sudden tears. "It's so beautiful," she finally whispered, her voice almost reverential.

Derek understood her reaction to the view more than she knew. "I feel the same way every time I ride these trails. There's something about the mountains and the views... it makes me feel closer to inner peace than anywhere else."

He cleared his throat, suddenly feeling vulnerable and a little laid bare, but Lacy nodded, her eyes clear and understanding.

"I get the feeling," she said softly, "that spending enough time out here would bring clarity. Answers to life's big questions."

"That's exactly it."

On impulse, Derek reached out and took her hand. It wasn't even a romantic impulse—he simply felt so connected to nature and, by extension, to her as well. Yet, as soon as he took her hand, even through the gloves, he felt a jolt of electricity shoot through him. They stared at each other and the scenery faded away, leaving only their eyes locked on each other as the tension between them thickened. Lacy swayed closer, as though pulled by a magnetic force, and Derek's body mirrored hers. Derek's breath caught in his throat but, even though everything in him wanted to lean down and kiss her, he knew it wasn't the time. So, as always, he turned to humor. Leaning down, he rubbed his nose against hers in an Eskimo kiss, making them both laugh and the tension faded a bit.

He led her back to the sled, but he wasn't ready for the date—or non-date, whatever it was—to end. "Are you hungry?"

"Ravenous."

"Good." Derek climbed on the sled behind her, but he had a thought before they took off. "Oh, and by the way, about ice skating? Our rink in town is run by the grouchiest man you'll ever come across. Only the bravest of heart actually go there. Trust me, in this town, you want to stick to dogsledding."

Lacy laughed, the clearness of it ringing through the chilly air. "And you know what? Now that I've had some experience, I don't mind that a bit."

CHAPTER FOURTEEN

Scooting her chair toward the table, Lacy ran her fingers through her hair, hoping she didn't look as windblown as she felt. As she did, she studied the little mom-and-pop restaurant Derek had taken her to. Frosty's Shack was a cozy place—what with its log cabin walls, the giant stone fireplace taking up most of one wall, and the scattered tables with their mismatched chairs. A stained-glass Tiffany lamp adorned the center of the table, emitting a soft yellow light and making their table feel intimate and warm.

"Derek and—Lacy, was it?—I'll have Becca come and take your orders shortly," Louise Thomas was saying.

Derek thanked her, and Louise threw them both a quick smile before hurrying off to the kitchen. Lacy watched her go, intrigued by the woman. Louise, the owner of Frosty's Shack, was a curious contradiction of businesslike and cozy. She wore her brown hair in a bun with a pencil stuck through it, paired with worn-out tennis shoes and a flowy skirt covered by a homemade apron, yet her manner was focused and efficient, although kind.

That was something Lacy was coming to appreciate about this town—most of the people she met were just... themselves. No facades, no pretenses, just authenticity.

Derek nudged a menu toward Lacy, although she noticed he didn't bother to open his. "Already know what you want?" she asked.

"Pretty much. I come here all the time, and I know all my favorite orders by heart."

Lacy rested her chin in her hand, taking in his chiseled features. Taking that ride through the New Hampshire landscape had changed something for her. She had been drawn to Derek from the start, but she now had a newfound admiration for him. He had built his own business from the ground up, and he was excellent at what he did. The businesswoman in her could appreciate that, but she knew it was more than that. Much as she'd been trying to ignore the pesky feelings of excitement that seemed to grow each time she was around him, she couldn't deny it any longer. Not after they had almost kissed on the mountain. No, like it or not, she was very much interested in Derek Morse.

"What are the best dishes here?"

"Definitely the chicken pot pie—I'm ordering that today, by the way. The pork roast and mashed potatoes, of course. Oh, and the homemade macaroni and cheese..." Derek groaned and patted his belly. "So, so good. No one does comfort food like Frosty's."

"You've converted me." Lacy closed her menu. "I'm copying you and getting the chicken pot pie. And a side of macaroni and cheese." She threw him a look. "And I don't want to hear about the calories or anything like that."

Derek raised his hands. "I'm the last person in the world who would comment on your food choices. I'm a firm believer in eating what feels good."

Lacy blinked a little, but she liked what he'd said. It was a far cry from some of the laser-focused finance guys she'd dated in the past, who had been obsessed with their looks and taking gym selfies, counting their carbs religiously, and giving her little judgmental stares when she ordered what she actually wanted instead of a salad or an egg-white omelet.

"Did I say something wrong?"

Lacy shook her head, a shy smile lifting the corners of her mouth. "Most definitely not," she said softly.

Their waitress, who Lacy guessed was Louise's daughter, based on their similar brown hair and outfits, came up just then to take their orders. Derek handed Becca their menus and told her his order, and Becca laughed when Lacy echoed his order exactly. On an impulse, feeling suddenly giddy and young, Lacy lifted a hand just when Becca was about to leave.

"Wait, could I get a hot chocolate as well? With whipped cream?"

Becca nodded, jotting down a note before promising to return with their food in a short time.

"Do you want some rainbow sprinkles to go with your hot choccy?" Derek cooed as Becca walked away.

Lacy stuck her tongue out. "Everyone loves hot chocolate with whipped cream!"

"Sure... when they're six."

Lacy folded her arms and raised an eyebrow. "Well, *some* of us actually like to enjoy life. So. I'm going to enjoy my 'hot choccy' and you'll just have to deal with it. And, if you start being nice to me, I might even share with you."

"My bad, my bad. I'm sure you're right."

"That's better," Lacy said with a sniff.

Derek tapped his long fingers on the wooden table, making the light from the little Tiffany lamp jump a little. "Now that you've actually gone out for a ride, has your mind changed about dogsledding being a pointless venture?"

Lacy pursed her lips, pretending to be offended. "Now, why on earth would you believe I thought that?"

Derek speared her with a knowing look that made the butterflies in her stomach flare up. "Maybe because it's been written all over your face, oh, I don't know—every single time dogsledding has come up."

Lacy couldn't stifle her laugh now and held up her hands in surrender. "Okay, fine, you got me," she admitted. "I didn't get it before, but my mind has definitely changed now. I think I finally see why you've devoted your life to your craft."

Derek smiled at her, his eyes lighting up at her words. "It really *is* a craft."

"And I know that now." Lacy toyed with the

napkin at her place setting. "It sounds really stuck-up to me now, even saying this out loud, but I didn't take it seriously. I guess I thought grown-ups sat at desks for their careers."

Derek shuddered, making her laugh. "Sitting at a desk day in and day out would be the death of me, but I know it works for some folks."

"Some folks like me, you mean?"

Derek shrugged. "Maybe?"

Lacy rested her chin in her hand again, thinking about it. "I think I don't mind it so much most of the time, but working on the mansion lately has been a nice break from paperwork and phone calls." She pulled a wry face then. "Well, I wouldn't say it's been a 'break', but you get the idea."

Becca returned carrying a tray with their food on it. She slid individual chicken pot pies in front of them, as well as a bowl of creamy macaroni and cheese and a mug of hot chocolate in front of Lacy, before slipping away. Lacy leaned over her food, inhaling the aromas from the steaming food with appreciation. Her mouth watered a little as she looked at the perfectly golden flaky crust of the pot pie and picked up her fork. Lacy dug in and took a bite, groaning with pleasure at the savory flavors and the buttery layers in the crust.

"Oh my gosh," she mumbled around her mouthful of food, lifting one hand to cover her mouth, "this is incredible."

"Told you," Derek said cheerfully, taking a bite of his own food. "Frosty's may look unassuming, but you can't beat it for taste."

"Amen," Lacy agreed fervently, taking a bite of her macaroni and cheese and feeling like she might be ascending to heaven. She lifted the mug of hot chocolate to her lips, taking a slow sip and feeling the warmth spread through her whole body. "You're missing out."

Derek cracked up and she glared at him.

"What?"

"I'm sorry, it's just..." He picked up his napkin and leaned across the table to dab at her mouth gently. "You had a whipped cream mustache."

Lacy felt herself begin to blush, but she didn't mind. Their eyes locked again, and that same electric tension that had swirled between them on the mountain returned. She realized that she too, was leaning across the table toward him. Blinking, she sat back, and the tension crackled and snapped before dissipating again.

She caught her breath, willing herself to inhale

and exhale normally. *Since when did breathing become so difficult?*

Louise returned to their table, a newspaper in hand. "I was just reading this in my office. Is it about you?"

Lacy leaned over to look at the newspaper and saw a picture of the old mansion before nodding. "Yes. A journalist asked me a while ago if he could write about it. I gave him some quotes."

"Can I see?" Derek reached for the paper, and Louise set it down. "Louise, do you mind if we borrow this? I'll return it, I promise."

"I know you will. I was supposed to be going over my ledger in the office, anyway. Take as long as you need."

Derek thanked her and then scooted his chair closer to Lacy's so they could read the article together. At first, Lacy couldn't concentrate, what with Derek's closeness. She could feel his breath against her neck as he leaned over her shoulder to read, but finally the words came together and she was able to make sense of them. The reporter had asked her about her relationship with Nicholas Spielman, and she had been forthcoming enough, mentioning Harv's bankruptcy due to corrupt business practices, and his and Nicholas's subsequent relocation to Snowy Pine Ridge. Derek stiffened as he read, then pushed the paper away.

"Derek, what's wrong?"

Derek moved his chair back into place and took a bite of his chicken pot pie, clearly needing a moment to gather his thoughts. His face was troubled. Lacy pushed her food away, suddenly losing all interest in her food. Had he decided he didn't want to be around someone with corrupt relatives? Did he think she was like them?

"What you said in the article about your father and Nicholas," Derek finally said. "Well, to be honest, it doesn't sit quite right with me."

Lacy wrinkled her brow. "What do you mean? That's what happened."

Derek nodded slowly, chewing the inside of his cheek, and Lacy noticed how pained his eyes were. "Look, I don't know what happened in your past, so I know it's not my place to cast judgment. I didn't know them back when you were a child."

Lacy gave a short laugh. "Well, that makes two of us."

"The thing is, Harv and Nicholas were really beloved in this town. I mean, folks around here called your grandfather St. Nick because he was such a generous man. I wouldn't even have my business if it wasn't for Nicholas and Harv helping me to get it financed." He hesitated. "How well did you know your grandfather?"

Lacy frowned, a ripple of surprise at Derek's admission running through her. *Winter Run Racing* existed because of her grandfather? And he was like some patron saint in Snowy Pine Ridge? She sighed, unsure of what to think.

"Like I said, I didn't really know him. All I know about my father and grandfather is what my mother told me growing up."

Derek looked at her, his eyes still pained, but now holding a new softness. "I'm sure she had her reasons."

Lacy nodded slowly. "She went through a lot after my dad went bankrupt and abandoned us."

Derek reached out and took her hand. "It sounds like you both did."

CHAPTER FIFTEEN

They finished the rest of their meal quietly, rarely speaking. Lacy's mind was a million miles away from her food, although she still took bites of her macaroni and cheese and chicken pot pie in a mechanical way. She certainly wasn't tasting the flavors that had pleased her only a few minutes earlier. Even Derek's presence couldn't draw her out of her swirling thoughts, but she appreciated in a detached sort of way how respectful he was of her sudden need for space to think. And think she did—questions about her father and grandfather, about her mother's version of events, about whether she had ever learned the whole truth—crowded against each other in her mind, pushing and pulling against each other in an endless internal debate. When Louise brought the check over to their table, Lacy tried to rouse herself from her inner storm.

"How was everything, you two?"

"It was perfect, as always, Louise," Derek responded, giving her a warm smile and reaching for the check.

Lacy reached for her purse. "Let me help."

Derek shook his head. "Like I said, my mother raised me to be a gentleman."

Lacy was too tired emotionally to argue. She gave him a wan smile and thanked him, then noticed that Louise was eying her a little askance.

"Was the food not to your liking?"

Lacy blinked, confused, but then she realized she had left the majority of her food on her plates. "No, Louise, everything was beyond delicious. I guess my eyes were bigger than my stomach today," she joked lamely, hoping Louise would buy it.

"A tiny little thing like you, it's no wonder," Louise responded, clearly appeased. "Let me get you a box for your leftovers."

When they were alone again, Lacy looked at Derek, who was studying her with worried eyes. For the briefest moment, she considered spilling the tangled mess in her mind to him, but then she quickly pulled back, stunned that the thought would

even occur to her. As much as she might like him—
and, at this point, she had to admit that she *did* like
him—she barely knew him. He had wanted a fun day
and she wasn't about to ruin it by dumping her
emotional baggage on him. Louise returned then
with a takeout box and wished them a good day. A
few moments later, Derek and Lacy were pulling on
their coats and gloves to leave Frosty's Shack.

"I didn't want to say anything with Louise
around," Derek said as the door of the restaurant
closed behind them, "but I feel like I need to
apologize."

Lacy wrinkled her brow. "For what? You didn't
do anything."

Derek stuffed his hands into the pockets of his
heavy winter coat, his auburn hair rustling in the
cold breeze. "I think I spoke out of turn in there and
put a damper on things... I hope I didn't ruin our fun
day by talking about Nicholas. It's clearly a sensitive
subject for you, and I should have respected that."

Lacy shook her head, mentally pushing away all
of the things that had arisen during their lunch and
locking them firmly away for the moment. She
smiled up at him. "Not at all. You didn't do anything
wrong." She pulled in a breath, but kept her smile in
place. "I was just... trying to reconcile the man I

thought I knew with the one you described to me." She shrugged. "Maybe I should've made an effort to get to know him while I still had the chance," she said, her voice softer now.

Derek took a small step closer, his eyes gentle. "If it's any comfort, I think you would've gotten along very well with Nicholas. And I can tell you one thing, for certain—he would have loved you."

Lacy blinked by sudden, unexpected tears and mustered up a watery smile, touched by his words. "Thanks." She blinked back the tears and tried to make a joke. "You have to say that because you just paid for my food, which I think makes this a date, and I know by now your mother raised you to be a gentleman."

To her surprise, Derek frowned, his eyes becoming more intense as they stared down into hers. The electric undercurrent between them began to buzz and snap once more.

"Lacy," he said, his voice lower and a little exasperated. "Do you have any idea how incredible you are?"

She froze, unable to shrug his words off with a joke, not when his gaze was boring into her and his words rang with sincerity.

"I knew and loved Nicholas, and I'd like to think

I'm starting to know you too," he continued. "I meant what I said before. He would have loved you, and..." He paused, hesitating. "And even if it's not my place to say it, I will. You would have been his whole world. I know it."

Lacy wasn't accustomed to feeling vulnerable in front of other people, but Derek had managed to bring that side out of her more than once by now. She stood before him, feeling laid bare, but she was surprised to find that it didn't feel threatening. Instead, she felt... seen.

The space between them seemed to evaporate, though neither had moved an inch. The cold, the street around them, all of it faded away, leaving just the two of them standing there. His eyes drifted from hers to her lips and then back again, and she wondered with bated breath.

Is he going to kiss me? She stood still, rooted to the spot. *Do I want him to? This is technically a date, but maybe he doesn't see it that way. Maybe he just sees me as an acquaintance.*

Her thoughts raced at dizzying speed, matching her heart beat, which had begun to thump at a pace she wasn't quite sure was healthy.

Before she could decide what she hoped would happen, Derek gave a tiny nod, almost to himself, and took a step back. The tension between them simmered down enough for her to catch her breath. Derek gave her an easy smile, seemingly unaffected by their moment, and she wondered for a brief second if she had imagined it all.

"I hope you had fun today. I know you weren't into the idea of dogsledding at first."

Lacy smiled back. "I really did have fun today. Thanks for taking me out on the trails."

"Any time, seriously. Once you've gone dogsledding once, you're hooked."

"I can see how that happens," Lacy said with a light laugh. "You know, I wasn't sure about coming to Snowy Pine Ridge in the first place, either, but I'm glad I did."

Derek's mouth quirked up in a lopsided grin. "This town has a way of sneaking up on you, that's for sure."

"I'm starting to realize that."

"I'm glad you made the leap, though," Derek said then, his gaze holding hers with that same intensity from before for the whisper of a heartbeat. "Snowy Pine Ridge wouldn't be the same without you."

The butterflies Derek always seemed to be sending into flight erupted in her stomach once more at those words. Hoping she looked calm and nonchalant, she gave him a little wave and thanked him again for a fun day before turning and heading down the street. As she walked toward the inn, she thought she could feel his gaze on her back. At the corner of the street, she dared to turn slightly to take a peek, and saw that he hadn't moved from his spot. Giving him one last wave, those butterflies flapping with all their might, she turned down the street and Frosty's Shack, and Derek with it, disappeared from sight.

* * *

The thought of returning to work on the house that afternoon held zero appeal for Lacy. When she got back to The Snowy Pine and safely into her bedroom, she undressed. Rather than pulling on her coveralls, she decided on a whim to draw a bath. In the quaint bathroom with its claw-foot tub and lacy curtains, she got the bath going, pouring in some of the complimentary Epsom salts sitting on the wooden tray that also held bubble bath, a candle, and a soap carved into the shape of a flower.

While the bath was filling, she donned a fluffy white robe and grabbed the bottle of wine she'd bought at Burkman's Grocery earlier that week. The grocery store had been a good place for her to grab some snacks and fixings to keep in the tiny kitchenette in her room—really just a mini-fridge hidden in a cabinet—for the times when she didn't want to eat at the inn or go to a restaurant. Uncorking the wine, she poured a generous glass for herself and, on impulse, grabbed her cell phone as well. She wanted to talk through the confusing web of her thoughts and feelings, and she hoped Madeline would have time even though it was the middle of the afternoon.

I would never do this back home, Lacy realized as she lowered herself into the warmth of the water. *I never had the time... or I guess, I never* let *myself take the time.*

She sighed with pleasure, wiggling a little as she got comfortable, and closed her eyes. The water soothed her, though her muscles had stopped aching as she'd gotten used to the physical labor of working on the mansion. No, the ache within her this time was emotional, not physical, but relaxing in her hotel room was already soothing away the thoughts that had plagued her at the restaurant.

She pulled in a deep breath then sank completely beneath the water, letting it envelop her completely and feeling, just for a moment, like she was weightless in the water. The sensation pleased her, so different from her usual feet-on-the-ground businesslike mentality. Coming back up for air, she decided to call Madeline. She felt more sure of herself now, less wounded and raw, but she still wanted to get her friend's take on everything. Drying one hand on the towel hanging by the bathtub, she reached for her phone. After hitting Madeline's contact, she pressed the speakerphone option and listened to the ringing fill the small bathroom. After a few rings, Madeline picked up, her greeting blaring and echoing off the bathroom walls. Wincing a little, Lacy adjusted the volume.

"Madeline, you'll never guess where I am right now."

"Well, I just finished up a *six hour* meeting with the *rudest* client, so literally wherever you are is better than here," Madeline grumped.

Lacy bit back a laugh. "Oh, you're going to kill me then. I'm soaking in a warm bath. In the middle of the afternoon. Just because I can."

Madeline groaned. "Ugh, you've got to be kidding me! Look at you, just living it up over there. You do realize I'm insanely jealous right now."

"I knew you would be," Lacy teased. "Why do you think I called you?"

"To rub it in that you've got this awesome vacation while some of us are still slogging it out in the corporate trenches."

"Yes, ma'am," Lacy cooed.

"Well, you sound so happy, Lace—I can't believe I'm going to say this, but have you ever thought about staying up there? I mean, you've got a mansion, so..."

Lacy's head jerked back a little at Madeline's unexpected comment and she gave a startled laugh. "Stay here? In Snowy Pine Ridge? I don't think so."

Even as the words left her mouth, Lacy felt a tiny tug in her chest that felt suspiciously like regret. Her life in St. Louis, while successful, was so... *busy*. Every moment. All the time. She barely had time to take care of herself, carving out a few hours once a week on Saturday mornings, and that no longer felt like enough. Besides, St. Louis was crowded, but it felt simultaneously lonely and isolating. Everyone hurried past each other, eager to get to where they were going. In Snowy Pine Ridge, everyone seemed to know each other, and warm greetings and long conversations seemed to be the norm. There was something appealing about that, especially since Madeline had lost all of her family.

What would it be like to always feel surrounded by warmth and love?

Lacy shook off the question, not ready to add another issue to the heavy thoughts that had come up at lunch. She decided to fill Madeline in on her date with Derek. "Remember when you asked me if I'd found some hot backwoods lumberjack?"

"Do I ever! And you brought up some hottie that races on sleds or something?"

"His name is Derek," Lacy reminded her, "and he's a dogsledder, but yes. So... he and I went on a date today. He took me dogsledding for the first time."

"Shut up! Did you actually enjoy that?"

"I didn't expect to, but it was actually really nice. On the mountain trails with all that fresh air and all the scenery—"

"And a hot guy's got his arms around you," Madeline interrupted, and Lacy laughed.

"Okay, I'll admit that didn't hurt."

"Well, it sounds way better than my dating life. I was supposed to meet up with some guy for drinks last night, but he stood me up. Never even bothered to text and tell me he wasn't going to be there."

"You're kidding," Lacy groaned. "Why do guys do that?"

"I shouldn't have gotten my hopes up. It's about par for the course with my other dating app experiences. Seriously, what *is* it with the men in this city? I always seem to match with hotshot finance bros that only care about themselves. They act like they're still frat boys in college, but they're in their forties! Come on!"

Lacy sank deeper into the tub, letting the water lap against her chin as she listened to Madeline talk about her woeful dating life. She could commiserate —she'd had her fair share of bad dates in St. Louis as well. Going out with Derek that day had been one of the best dates she'd ever had, and she knew it wasn't just because Derek was an incredible guy. Seeing more of the scenery in the mountains, trying out a local restaurant, simply being in Snowy Pine Ridge... well, she was starting to realize how special this town was, which was something she had never anticipated.

I may only be here for a short time, she thought, wiggling her toes in the water, *but I'm going to enjoy every minute that I'm here.*

CHAPTER SIXTEEN

After mulling it over for a solid week, Colette had finally come to a decision. It was the article in the newspaper that clinched the decision for her, really —she was going to seek out Lacy Preston and invite her to meet Emma. She hadn't told Emma about her decision, of course, but she figured in this case it was best to ask for forgiveness rather than permission.

Friday afternoon, after Emma had settled in her room for her daily afternoon nap, Colette had shrugged on her coat and quietly left the house. At first she had considered going to The Snowy Pine, but that felt too intimate. It was there as a last resort, but she had heard around town, as well as from Derek, that Lacy liked to hang out with Sarah at

Sweet Thing Bakery. Crossing her fingers and hurrying down the sidewalk, shoulders hunched against the freezing wind, Colette paused by the entrance to the bakery. Although she knew she had every right to go in, she felt a little guilty, like something of a stalker.

It's for a good cause, she reasoned with herself. *Do it for Emma.*

Taking one last steadying breath, Colette pushed open the door.

Relief, mingled with a good dose of nerves, poured over her as she saw Lacy's telltale short honey-brown hair. Lacy was tapping away on her laptop, which was resting on the front counter of the bakery. After a moment she beamed, gesturing enthusiastically to Sarah and turning her laptop so Sarah could see the screen as well. Neither woman had noticed her yet, and Colette took the opportunity to take a step closer and squint at the screen as well. Pictures of gorgeous and decadent Victorian rooms filled the screen.

Maybe that's a good sign. Maybe it means she is planning to restore Nicholas's mansion to its former glory.

At that moment, Sarah looked up and saw her,

interrupting Colette's thoughts and sending nervous energy shooting through her limbs.

"Colette, hi! It's good to see you out and about! I know you're usually busy with Emma, so this is a pleasant surprise." Sarah's smile was huge and, as always, radiated with a bubbly warmth. "I'm going to flatter myself and say that you stopped by to sample my newest creation—red velvet brownies with white chocolate chips. They're to *die* for, promise!"

"I'll bet," Colette responded with a smile, although she didn't tell Sarah that in her anxious state the thought of a sugary treat made her queasy. She took a deep breath and turned to look at Lacy, who was watching the interchange with mild interest. "Actually, I came to meet you. You're Lacy Preston, aren't you?"

Lacy smiled with a warmth Colette hadn't been expecting. "I am! It seems just about everyone in this town knows who I am before I meet them," she said with a laugh.

"It's a small town, so word gets around," Sarah interjected. "Even over to Emma's tucked away cottage."

"Derek came by for a visit," Colette said hastily, not wanting to lose her nerve. "He told me about

Nicholas leaving you the mansion, and then, of course, I read the article in the paper."

Lacy's face stilled ever so slightly at the mention of the article and Colette felt her stomach clench. Everything in her wanted to run—after all, she was peace-loving and averse to conflict—but she had come too far now to just walk away. Nicholas's memory deserved better than that. Emma, as his former love, deserved better than that too.

There's no time to be a coward, she told herself. *It's now or never.*

"Lacy," Colette said, and her lips felt a little numb as she spoke. "I actually wanted to talk to you about that article..."

Lacy's mouth pinched into a tight line and it was all Colette could do not to turn tail and run.

"I... er... well, I read it and... and... well, I don't think you got it right," she finally blurted at the end of her stammering sentence.

"In what way?" Lacy's words were clipped off through clenched teeth. Colette felt a hot flush of mortification spreading up her neck and consuming her cheeks.

"I'm sorry, I'm not explaining myself well..." Stuffing her now-trembling hands into her coat pockets, she tried once more. "When I was reading the article, I just felt that... some things you said about Nicholas weren't correct. Maybe you didn't have all the facts about your grandfather, and no one can blame you for that," she added quickly, as one of Lacy's eyebrows arched high. "Did you know him well?"

Lacy folded her arms tightly, drawing herself up. "I don't see how that's any of your business," she said, and her icy tone sent a chill through Colette. "I don't think you have any right to interrogate me in this way, to be quite frank."

Sarah was wringing her hands together behind the counter. "Ladies, maybe we should sit down..."

Lacy softened a bit, tucking a strand of her hair behind her ear and sending Sarah a weak smile. "It's fine, Sarah." She blew out a breath. "Look, I don't mean to be so defensive, but it seems like everyone around here has an opinion on Nicholas, and it's far different from what I've known my whole life. Derek made that more than clear the other day," she added, sounding a bit grumpy now, as though the memory still rankled her.

Colette clutched onto that utterance like a drowning woman to a lifeline. "Derek! He's my cousin, actually."

That pulled Lacy up short. "He is?"

Colette nodded hard, then forced herself to stop when she realized she must look like a crazed bobblehead. "Yes. That's part of why I wanted to talk to you. Derek was really close to Nicholas, as I'm sure you know by now. I also work for Emma Cleaver—she and Nicholas were in a relationship, and she's taken his passing pretty hard."

"I see," Lacy said, her voice softer now. She slumped against the counter, clearly mulling over this new piece of information.

"I was wondering if you'd be willing to come and talk to Emma," Colette continued, relieved that the worst was over now. "I just think she might be able to show you a side of your grandfather that maybe you never knew about. And I'm sure she'd want to meet you—Nicholas talked about you so much."

Lacy blinked, looking a bit stunned. It was a far cry from her icy defensiveness only moments before. She hesitated, and Colette took a step forward, taking advantage of the moment.

"Please, Lacy. If not for your grandfather, then for a lonely woman who is grieving right now."

Lacy closed her eyes with a sigh and Colette held her breath, forcing herself to wait. A moment later, her patience was rewarded.

"Fine," Lacy said, her voice tinged with a

grumble. "How about tomorrow morning, around ten?"

"Thank you," Colette breathed, backing away before Lacy could change her mind. "I'll let Sarah give you the address," she tossed over her shoulder, hurrying out of the bakery and back into the cold.

* * *

"Sounds good, Brenda," Lacy said into her cell phone. "Keep me posted, okay?"

After Brenda promised to do so, Lacy ended the call with her assistant and pocketed her phone, turning back to scan the shelf in front of her. She'd spent the rest of the afternoon after the conversation with Colette running errands— touching base with Brenda and some of her clients, ordering some more cleaning supplies and paint at Mitchell Hardware, and now picking up some items at the local grocery store. Despite keeping busy, the conversation at the bakery had played over and over in her mind, hovering in an endless loop behind her forced busyness.

"Can I help you find anything?"

Lacy jumped a little at the unexpected voice and

whirled to see a worker watching her. Lacy mustered up a smile.

"No, I'm fine, thank you."

"If you *do* need anything..."

"I'll be sure to find you," Lacy promised.

The worker smiled, then drifted away and Lacy turned back to the shelf of beauty products in front of her. The selection was much smaller than back in St. Louis, and her usual brands weren't present. Picking a can of hairspray at random, she tossed it into her basket, then threw in a tube of mascara and a bottle of facial cleanser before making her way up to the front and getting in line at one of the cash registers. Christmas music played over the store's speakers, and someone had put up a tree near the sliding front doors. Some of the tension that had sat with her all day eased a little as she let herself take in her surroundings.

By the time she paid for her items and stepped out into the cold, however, the tension had returned. Suddenly, the thought of returning to her room at The Snowy Pine, cozy as it was, held little appeal for her. On impulse, she turned and began walking in the direction of Derek's shop. She knew it was ridiculous to even walk in that direction, but she couldn't deny that a part of her hoped he would be in his shop working and ask her to stay and talk. And if he did, she knew she would accept.

As she approached Winter Run Racing in the fading evening light, she saw that a light still burned within the shop. She cupped her hands around her eyes and peeked through the massive front window, but didn't see Derek in the main room of the shop, although a dogsled with tools strewn about it still sat in the middle of the floor, as though he had just paused his repairs for a quick break. Before she could talk herself out of it, she tested the doorknob on impulse. When it twisted with ease, she pushed open the door and stepped inside, walking toward the back of the room where light spilled under the crack of a closed door. As she approached, she heard the soft yips of several dogs.

Pulling the door open a crack, she was met by the sight of an enormous room filled with kennels, but not like any kennels she'd seen before. Mouth opening a bit, she ventured inside, swiveling her head to take it all in. Large kennels, larger than any she'd seen before, lined the walls, each holding fluffy dog beds, dog toys, and soft blankets.

It's like a posh hotel for dogs, she marveled to herself, taking it all in.

Dogs flopped on their beds, nuzzled into

blankets, chewed on bones, and yipped at each other —all clearly at home and comfortable as could be.

Just then, Derek entered through a door at the back of the kennel room, carrying a large bag of dog food on his shoulder. He paused mid-step as he saw her, and Lacy was suddenly aware of how crazy she must look. After all, she'd let herself into his shop and wandered at will.

I look like a stalker, breaking and entering like this, she groaned inwardly.

To her relief, Derek grinned at her, not seeming too alarmed by her presence.

"Just couldn't stay away, I see," he teased, slinging the bag off his shoulder and setting it on the ground.

"I'm here for the dogs," she teased back, entirely relieved that he hadn't kicked her out on sight or probed more deeply into her reason for showing up unannounced. She wanted to talk about it, but she wasn't sure where to begin.

"In that case, let me introduce you."

Derek sidled over to her and pointed to the gorgeous husky in the kennel nearest her. "That magnificent fellow is Bartholomew."

"Bartholomew?" Lacy sputtered and laughed at the same time.

"But we just call him Bart," Derek said blithely, refusing to be baited as she dissolved into laughs. "And in the next kennel we have two sisters—Lucky and Daisy."

"They're so cute," Lacy breathed, crouching down to study them. The two sisters were curled up around each other, their sides rising and falling as they slumbered peacefully.

"And you've already met Missy," Derek continued, leading Lacy to the next kennel.

Missy jumped up against the kennel's bars and Lacy unlatched the door, taking the puppy into her arms. Missy covered her in kisses as Lacy snuggled her close.

"Who's a good girl? Are you a good girl?" Lacy asked, cooing into the puppy's fur.

"She's a handful," Derek said with a smile, his eyes soft, "but she is indeed a very good girl."

"Of course she is. Aren't you, baby? Yes, you are."

Derek laughed as Missy wriggled out of Lacy's arms and trotted back into her kennel to begin chewing at a squeaky toy with intense energy. He closed the door behind her. "She's like this about 90% of the time."

"Like you said, all that energy will come in handy once she gets the hang of sledding."

"It definitely will." Derek raised his arm. "Come on, let me introduce you to the others."

Over the next ten minutes or so, Derek introduced Lacy to each and every dog from his teams. As they walked and met the dogs, Lacy marveled over and over again at the bond between Derek and his dogs. It was plain as day that they all adored him, and Lacy was struck once again at seeing Derek in his element.

This man is doing exactly what he should be doing with his life, she thought, her heart swelling with wonder.

"They all respond to you so well," she commented.

"I would hope so," he said with a chuckle. "Out on the trail, the team and the driver have to respect and trust each other. I spend a lot of time selecting and training my teams, and we get pretty attached to each other."

"Do you ever have to give any away?"

"At times. I have a pretty extensive and lengthy selection process when I home a trained sled dog with a dogsled owner. They have to be licensed, obviously, but I spend a good bit of time vetting the potential owners to make sure they're worthy of these amazing dogs." He frowned and leaned against the wall, looking down at her. "You know, this industry gets a bad reputation—people talk about animal abuse and how this sport is cruel to animals."

"I don't think anyone who has seen you with your teams could ever call you abusive."

"I would hope not. I treat all of my dogs with love and respect, and if a dog doesn't love the trails or take to sledding, I spend a lot of time finding them a good home." His gaze intensified, his eyes searching hers. "This work is my life. I want to do it well."

"I'll admit I didn't know much about it before I came here, but I'm glad I know now. I'm sure there will always be people in any profession that abuse their power and give others a bad name, but you're not one of them." On impulse, she reached out and brushed his hand with hers for just a moment, before taking it back. Suddenly embarrassed, she changed the subject. "I met Colette today," she blurted.

Derek blinked a little, but he didn't seem to mind the topic change. "She's great, isn't she? How did the two of you meet?"

"Well, she came to the bakery today while I was talking to Sarah. She... said that she had a problem with what I said about Nicholas in the newspaper article. Apparently she wants me to meet with some woman named Emma so they can set the record straight."

Derek cocked his head to the side, his forehead wrinkling. "She said it like that?"

Lacy colored a little and blew out a breath. "Well, no. She was really nice about it... I just might not have taken it all with good grace."

"Hey, it's understandable. I know this is a sensitive subject for you." He looked at his feet for a moment, and when he spoke again his voice was soft. "For what it's worth, I think talking to Emma would be a good thing. I don't know what happened between you and Nicholas, but I think there might be some misunderstandings there."

Lacy folded her arms, ready to be defensive again, but she just found she couldn't. Instead, she leaned against the wall too, and closed her eyes. "Everything I've done in my life—my career, my education, all of it—it's all been to distance myself from Nicholas and my father. I was always told they were dishonorable, and I never wanted to be like them."

"I can't imagine what that must've felt like for you," Derek whispered, reaching out and taking her hand.

She laced her fingers through his but didn't open her eyes. "It was awful, but it pushed me to work hard. It's my whole identity."

When Derek hesitated, she finally opened her eyes and saw that he was watching her with an expression so tender it almost broke her heart.

"Lacy," he whispered. "You've worked so hard, and that's admirable."

"Thank you."

"But... but I don't think your work should define you. Or what your father and grandfather did or didn't do."

"I'm not sure I know any other way," she admitted, and tears began to sting the back of her throat.

Derek put a finger under her chin and guided her to look back up at him. "Over the past week, I've seen so many different sides to you, and if there's one thing I know, it's that you're brave. You came to a town you've never heard of, have taken on the repairs of a mansion, and"—his eyes danced— "you even went sledding with me. So, knowing that, I know that you can be brave again and learn more about your grandfather. You're brave and open-minded and it's a beautiful side of you."

The tightness that had coiled itself in Lacy's

chest the entire afternoon began to loosen as she listened to him speak.

"I don't know if I'm *that* open-minded," she murmured.

"You can be, though," he whispered. "I truly believe it."

CHAPTER SEVENTEEN

"Do you want me to come in with you?"

Lacy glanced over at Derek, who was watching her from the driver's side of his truck. She shook her head. Her stomach had been in knots after she'd left Derek's the previous night and had gone back to the inn. He had been kind and offered her a ride to Emma's house, and she'd gratefully accepted, but she knew that whatever was going to happen inside that house was something she needed to face on her own. She shifted slightly to look out the window at Emma's house—a charming stone cottage with an arched front door in a deep blue that normally would have taken her fancy. Today, though, that charm was entirely lost on her. All she could think about was what might wait for her within. She wasn't just worried about what Emma might say, she was also worried about the reception she might receive. Colette had seemed nice enough the previous day, but this Emma Cleaver had been Nicholas's girlfriend, and she surely would not have appreciated Lacy's contribution to the newspaper article.

"Lacy? Are you sure you'll be all right?"

Lacy pulled her eyes away from Emma's cottage and mustered up a tremulous smile. "I'm fine, really. Just got lost in my thoughts for a second."

Derek looked skeptical, but he finally nodded. "Just know that I'm always here."

Even though it had been little more than a week or two since she'd arrived in Snowy Pine Ridge, Lacy was surprised to realize that she *did* know that. Her racing heart settled a little and her smile became genuine. "I know, and I'm grateful for it. I'll be in touch, okay?"

"Good luck." Derek reached over and squeezed her hand gently, the way one friend would to comfort another. "Remember how we talked about bravery and open-mindedness last night? That's what's going to carry you through today, I promise."

Lacy realized vaguely that she should be uncomfortable with his pep talk. After all, she had next to no one in her life that bolstered her confidence or shared the mental load with her. To her surprise, however, she found it was nice to feel like she had someone on her team, instead of flying solo. With newfound resolve, Lacy opened the truck door and hopped to the ground, then looked back up at Derek.

"Thanks again," she said softly, then waved. "Now, get out of here before I change my mind and get back in the truck."

"Yes, ma'am," he replied, giving her a salute.

She shut the truck door and stepped back to watch as he backed out of the driveway and drove down the lane that led back into town. Taking in a deep breath for courage, she turned and faced Emma's cottage. Not giving herself time to overthink things again, she marched up the front steps and rapped on the front door. A moment later, Colette opened the door. She stepped back, making space for Lacy to enter, and Lacy noticed that she looked far less timid now that she was back in her element.

"I'm so glad you came," Colette said, helping Lacy with her coat and hanging it on a coat stand. "Emma's waiting for you in the living room."

Colette led the way into a cozy room with a large stone fireplace, flanked by two cushy armchairs with a plush sofa facing them. Emma sat in one of the armchairs, her wrinkled hands folded together on her lap. Lacy studied her secretly as she took a seat on the sofa. Emma was an elderly woman with fluffy white hair pulled back into a banana clip. Reading glasses dangled from a chain around her neck and, for some reason, Lacy found that particular detail reassuring. Colette settled into the armchair opposite Emma's, and the three sat in awkward silence for a few moments.

Tension began to gather in Lacy's chest, and she wondered who was supposed to speak first. Forcing herself not to fidget, she reminded herself sternly that she was a successful businesswoman who had faced situations that were far more tense.

Come on, you've never been one to sit in the back seat and wait. Pull yourself together and take charge.

With that bracing thought, Lacy cleared her throat and leaned forward.

"Emma, it's nice to meet you. I'm Lacy Preston, as I'm sure you already know."

"Yes, dear, I do know," Emma answered, nodding.

When she didn't say anything further, Lacy realized she would have to bring up the reason they were all gathered and address the proverbial elephant in the room.

"Well, then. Colette brought it to my attention yesterday that neither of you agree with what I said about Nicholas in the newspaper article." Lacy glanced at Colette, who was now chewing the side of her lip, her forehead wrinkled with worry.

Well, at least I'm not the only one feeling uncomfortable.

"I know what I've been told my whole life," she continued, taking a deep breath and reminding herself to keep an open mind, "but I'm here to listen to your side of the story."

"That's very commendable, dear," Emma said after a long moment that left Lacy second-guessing herself. She reached across the small space and patted Lacy's knee, then settled back against her chair. "Oh, my... where to begin..."

Colette and Lacy sat in respectful silence, allowing Emma time to gather her thoughts. Emma's eyes became dreamy as she drifted down memory lane, her thoughts clearly a million miles away.

"I can still remember the first time I met Nicholas," she finally began, and her voice was soft as velvet, tender with the recollection. "I was at the farmers market sorting through the plums, when the kindest looking man I'd ever seen beckoned me over to him. He told me the best plums actually came from Briarberry Farms, who had a booth down the row, and he offered me his arm to walk me down to their booth. I put my hands on my hips and asked just who he thought he was telling me I didn't have perfect plum-picking skills." Emma's eyes shone and she laughed at the memory. "He didn't mind my spitfire at all, though, and he told me I looked like a woman who deserved the sweetest things in life, and that included finding the perfect plums."

To her surprise, Lacy found herself softening as she listened to Emma's memory, but then she pulled herself up short.

Just because he knew how to flirt doesn't mean he was a good man, she told herself. *If anything, it shows just what a practiced con-artist he was.*

In the very next breath, though, Lacy could hear Derek's voice in her ear, reminding her to keep an open mind about the grandfather she had never really known. Squashing her uncharitable thoughts, she focused on Emma again and listened.

"That was after his wife—your sweet grandmother, my dear—had passed away. He and I became good friends after that chance meeting at the farmers market, and he courted me in the old-fashioned way. He would come sit with me in the evenings and we would talk for hours. Oh, and he planned the most thoughtful outings—museums, picnics, dinners." Emma lifted one hand and rested it on her heart, a few tears gathering in the corners of her eyes. "He was the kindest and most thoughtful man I have ever known."

Lacy felt a lump swell in her throat. These recollections felt too personal, and she felt like an undeserving outsider getting to see a moment meant to be private. When Emma lapsed into reminiscent silence, Colette eventually picked up a photo album resting on the table beside her chair and handed it to Emma. The album pulled Emma back to the present, and she took it, bestowing a kindly smile on Colette.

"Ah, yes, thank you for reminding me." Emma opened the album, running a wrinkled finger over the first page of photos before turning it to show Lacy. "I made it a project to capture the special impact that Nicholas and your father, Harv, had on this town. Oh, there were so many businesses in Snowy Pine Ridge and the surrounding towns that wouldn't have made it without their help, so I thought I would gather photos for Nicholas, as a gift." She nodded, sagely, turning the page and glancing at more photos. "Would you like to see it, Lacy? They provided financing for so many hopeful business owners, making their dreams come true."

Lacy took the album and began perusing the pictures, trying to hide how the images of her father and grandfather felt like a knife to the heart. All of these photos of them smiling with strangers she didn't know, all when they had abandoned her and her mother. How many nights had she cried herself to sleep as a little girl, missing her father so much she could barely breathe? Anger flared through her and she slammed the album shut. Emma and Colette jumped a little, stunned by her reaction.

Lacy found it hard to speak around the burning lump in her throat. "If they were doing so well with their businesses, why didn't they ever reach out to me? Harv and Nicholas left me and my mother alone to fend for ourselves! And all those businesses they 'helped'? I'm sure they were using business dealings just as shady as what led to my father's bankruptcy in the first place."

Emma leaned forward, reaching for Lacy's hand. "Oh, my dear, how you must have hurt for so many years..."

Emma's tenderness almost broke Lacy, and a tear slid down her cheek. Almost angrily, she swiped it away. "I became stronger because of it. I just don't understand how they could be so selfish and abandon a little girl like that."

"But they didn't," Emma said softly, waiting until Lacy met her gaze. She squeezed Lacy's hand. "Nicholas tried over and over throughout the years to contact you, to tell you the truth about what happened. You see, I'm afraid you never got the full story, and I'm afraid no one ever told you that they didn't go bankrupt because of any dishonest business practices."

Lacy swiped away another tear even as her chin trembled. "How can that be? My mother told me that my entire life."

"Because she was angry," Emma whispered. "We can never know why she could not forgive your father for going bankrupt, but you need to know that he and Nicholas were not dishonest men. And I meant it. Nicholas tried so very many times to contact you, but your mother must not have told you."

Lacy dropped her head into her hands, her mind whirling with the implications of this new information.

No. It can't be. She refused to accept it as true.

"That's impossible," she finally said, her voice ragged.

Emma patted her knee. "Nicholas wrote to you so many times, and he has a box he left for you. It's here in the house and I've been looking for it. The only problem is that it's locked, although Nicholas assured me that you would be able to open it. He said he left you a key."

Lacy looked at Emma through watery eyes, Emma's image distorting through the teardrops that almost blinded her. "No, he never left me a—"

She stopped speaking abruptly as a long-buried memory came floating back to her. When she was just a little girl, she remembered that one year for her birthday, Nicholas had presented her with a necklace on which hung a beautiful and ornate key. She had worn the key necklace proudly for years, rubbing it and studying it when she felt lonely, but after he and her father had left, she had never worn it again. Could it really be that Nicholas had handed her the key to this box so many years ago?

"Ah, so you do remember," Emma murmured. "My dear, I will do all I can to remember where the box is and present it to you. I just know that it will change everything."

Lacy wrapped her arms around her middle as though she could hold herself together and a spark of hope blossomed in her heart, a spark that she thought had died for good when her heart had been broken as a little girl. Opening her heart again like this, daring to hope that she had not truly been abandoned, could be foolish. What if she was just setting herself up for more heartbreak?

Bravery, she reminded herself. *Bravery and an open mind.*

"I want to believe you," she finally said. "But I need to see what's in that box first to understand."

"And that is why I shall not rest until I find it. I promise you that."

Lacy nodded. She realized that she wanted to know more about this man she had spent so many years hating. Almost shyly, she asked, "Can you tell me more about Nicholas?"

Emma smiled. "With pleasure. Let's see... Nicholas used to throw the most magnificent parties every year on Christmas Eve. Oh, if only you could have seen them."

Emma's eyes were alight with joy as she spoke of the music and dancing, the enormous Christmas tree in the front parlor, the rooms packed with townspeople, the garlands twisting around the grand staircase. In spite of herself, Lacy felt herself becoming wrapped up in the magic of it all.

"They were the grandest parties, and everyone looked forward to them. There's a reason he was called St. Nick, you know," Emma said, nodding.

"Oh, what I wouldn't give to see the old place like that again..."

Emma continued reminiscing, but Lacy barely heard her. Instead, her thoughts were off and racing. Emma's simple pronouncement had given Lacy an idea...

CHAPTER EIGHTEEN

Derek forced himself not to sprint down the street the way he wanted to, keeping his legs moving at a rapid speed-walk instead. After a couple of days of radio silence from Lacy—he hadn't talked to her since he'd dropped her off at Emma's house—she had finally reached out that morning, asking if he could meet up for lunch at Frosty's Shack.

She'd said she needed to discuss something important with him, and the clipped tone of her text exuded the urgency of her message.

Of course, he'd texted back right away, telling her that he would meet her then, but that he was also free before if she needed him. She'd said lunch would be fine, and he'd had to accept her answer. With no further information, but thrumming with nerves about what could be wrong, the minutes until their planned lunch had seemed to crawl by.

Pushing open the door of the cafe, Derek searched for Lacy almost frantically, his breath caught in his throat. After the glaring brightness of the sun reflecting on the snow outside, it took his eyes a moment to adjust to the softer light within Frosty's Shack. Lacy looked up from her perch in a cozy corner booth and raised a hand in greeting.

To Derek's surprise, her eyes were alight with excitement, and her air was one of focused, yet not frantic, energy. Confused, he made his way toward her, fighting to control his breathing, which had been coming in little puffs by the time he'd made it to the restaurant.

"Lacy, you're all right?"

Lacy raised an eyebrow, looking confused. "Yes. Why wouldn't I be?"

Derek dropped into the booth across from her, blowing out a breath and laughing a little. "And here I thought we were in some kind of emergency mode."

Lacy looked bewildered. "Why in the world would you think that?"

"Maybe because you sent me a text early this morning saying you needed to meet with me and that it was urgent."

"If I recall correctly, I said it was 'important' not that it was 'urgent'."

Derek flushed a little and rolled his eyes with a chuckle. "Okay, but it came across as urgent. I've been worried sick!"

"Aww, you were worried sick about me?" Lacy tossed him a teasing grin that just about stopped his heart, although this time it had nothing to do with his earlier worries for her. "Seriously, though, I'm sorry I alarmed you. Sometimes when I get caught up in my work I'm a terrible texter and I miss cues that, you know, a normal human would notice."

"Yeah, I got that," Derek commented dryly. He leaned forward then, unable to rake her over the coals any longer and nodded at her open laptop. "So? What's going on that's so important?"

Lacy leaned forward, all excitement, ready to talk, when Becca came up to the table bearing two glasses of water with lemon wedges. "Oh, I wasn't sure what you'd want to drink, so I just ordered water for you."

"That's fine," Derek replied, entirely past the point of caring about what he would be drinking.

"Have you decided what you want to order?" Becca asked, setting down their drinks.

"Um... I'll have whatever the special of the day

is," Derek replied, still distracted. "Lacy?"

"Same for me."

"Okay, I'll have that out to you in a jiffy."

Derek rested his elbows on the table, leaning forward, giving Lacy his full attention. Lacy turned the laptop so he could see the screen as well. Images of grand Victorian–style rooms filled with guests in evening wear filled the screen. He studied the pictures, then looked up at her. Lacy was practically buzzing with excitement, but for no reason he could understand.

"Well?"

"Um... these are really pretty pictures."

Lacy laughed. "I guess I should've given you some context."

"Context is good, yeah."

"Okay, so I've been thinking. When I was at Emma's house, she mentioned that Nicholas would throw huge parties at the mansion every Christmas Eve. She went on and on about the music and the dancing and the decorations..."

Comprehension began to dawn for Derek, but he let Lacy continue, since she was clearly in her element now.

"Well, what if I were to throw the party this year? We could have sled races outside, music and dancing of course, and we could even have some booths in the front hall so local businesses like Sweet Thing could sell their wares."

She paused to take in a breath and, suddenly looking a little vulnerable, tucked her hair behind her ears.

"I don't know what will happen to the mansion afterward," she continued. "I mean, I have some liquid savings, but not enough to get the place on its feet as an actual event venue without looking into business loans or cashing in some of my investments, but... I don't know, it could be worth a try, right? When I show folks just how good the mansion is starting to look and throw a lavish party, they might see it with new eyes. Or, at least, that's the hope." She paused again, flushing a little. "Derek, please say something. Why aren't you saying anything? What are you thinking?"

Derek gave her a half-grin. "I haven't said anything because my mother raised me right and I know it's rude to interrupt someone when they're speaking," he teased, pleased when she relaxed and laughed. "In all seriousness, though, I think it's a fantastic idea."

"Really?"

"I really do. Everyone loved the parties Nicholas

would throw, and I know everyone in town would be beyond excited to attend another one, especially since you've been getting the mansion restored to its former glory."

"And do you think they'd consider it as a viable venue for other events? Wedding receptions, galas, all of that?" Lacy looked vulnerable again. "I don't usually feel this unsure of myself. I'm used to running my own business, but all of this... well, it's personal for me this time."

Derek reached out and took her hand. "And that's why it's going to be perfect. I have no doubt whatsoever that the mansion would make an incredible venue."

Lacy blew out a breath that Derek suspected she'd been holding. "Thanks. That means a lot." She suddenly sat up straight. "Oh, I can't believe I almost forgot to tell you! When I was talking to Emma the other day, she said that Nicholas left a box for me in her care. She's still looking for it, but apparently it's locked and my grandfather left me the key."

Derek raised his eyebrows. "Wow. Do you know where the key is?"

"It's on a necklace he gave me when I was a little girl. It's somewhere back in St. Louis—I haven't worn it since my father left us."

"How do you feel about all of this?"

Lacy shrugged one shoulder. "I'm not sure... part of me wants to know more about him, especially if I was wrong about him all these years."

Derek squeezed her hand. "I'm glad you're learning more about him."

Lacy nodded, looking a little surprised at herself. "Me too."

Just then, Becca emerged from the kitchen carrying a tray with two steaming plates of pork roast, mashed potatoes with gravy, and sauteed green beans. She slid the plates in front of them, cautioning them that the food was hot, and then slipped away again. Derek let go of Lacy's hand and picked up his fork, suddenly ravenous and realizing he hadn't eaten all day, what with worrying about Lacy.

"Shall we?" he asked, lifting his glass of water to clink it against hers.

"Cheers." She laughed, then picked up her fork.

* * *

Colette stood up, putting her hands against the small of her back and arching as far as she could. A low groan escaped her as she did so, and she sagged a bit after the stretch. She had been digging through the attic for hours now, and she was almost certain by the grumbling from her stomach that it had to be nearly dinnertime. She closed the chest of old clothes she'd been searching through, sneezing as a puff of dust floated through the air.

It's unlikely the box is even in the attic, seeing as how Emma can't come up here herself, she thought, but she knew she would have to look through every nook and cranny of the dusty attic anyway.

Emma wouldn't be able to rest until she found the box, and Colette was worried about Emma's health. The elderly woman had been pushing herself for days on end now, looking through dusty corners and the back of every closet in the house. If they didn't find the box soon, Colette was afraid of what it might do to Emma.

She had long since begun to worry that the box wasn't even in the house, but Emma was insistent that Nicholas had, in fact, brought it to her and that she had definitely stowed it away somewhere within the cottage's walls.

But what if Emma is remembering it wrong?

Colette shoved the thought away, knowing that it would do no good to try reasoning with Emma once more. It only made things worse. No, the best thing she could do was to keep searching. The faster they found it, the sooner Emma would get to rest and stop wearing herself out on this seemingly futile quest.

With a sigh, Colette bent her still-aching back and dug into the next chest, this one full of old papers and mementos. Her movements were mechanical by now after so much searching, and her mind had begun to wander when she heard a faint shout coming from somewhere in the house. Instantly, Colette sprang to her feet and raced down the attic stairs, her heart in her throat.

"Emma? Emma? Are you all right? Did you get hurt?"

"I'm fine, dear," Emma called back.

It sounded as though her voice was coming from the bedroom. Colette hurried down to the first floor of the home and into Emma's room to find Emma sitting on the edge of her bed, a locked wooden box resting on her lap. Colette pulled up short, reaching out to hold the door frame for support.

"Is that...?"

Emma looked up at her, eyes filled with happy tears. "It is," she confirmed, her voice almost reverent. "We found it. We finally found Nicholas's box."

Colette came into the room then and sat beside Emma, staring at the box that had given Emma so much cause for worry. "Where was it? I swear we've poked through every dusty corner of this house three times over."

"Well," Emma said with a chuckle, "that's because it wasn't in a dusty corner at all. I found it at the bottom of my quilting basket."

"Your quilting basket?"

"Yes, dear. I remember now I had put it there because I thought I would see it all the time and never forget where it was. The thing is, though, we've only been knitting for the last couple of months—"

"Because of the blanket donation," Colette finished for her, understanding dawning on her. Suddenly the hilarity of the situation hit her with full force, and she flopped backward on the bed, overcome with laughter. "Oh my word, it was in the quilting basket the whole time!"

Emma's shoulders shook with laughter. "After all this trouble, it was sitting right beside my bed this whole time!"

Colette sat up, wiping away tears, her laughter finally subsiding. "Oh my, the messes we get into. At least now you can finally rest."

"Oh, no, dear, not yet. No, this box needs to go to its rightful owner."

CHAPTER NINETEEN

Lacy was coming to love the smell of fresh paint. It was never something she'd really considered before, but as she'd worked on the mansion day in and day out for the past couple of weeks, it had taken on almost a perfume-like quality, symbolizing fresh starts and a job well done. She dipped her roller brush back into the painting tray, which was currently full of the shade Fresh Cream for the dining room. It was a delicate off-white color that evoked warmth and cleanliness, and it was already making the room feel bigger than it had before.

Humming softly to herself, she began rolling another portion of the wall, leaning into the task and losing herself in the predictable rhythm of it. She'd hardly expected to enjoy the tasks required to resurrect the mansion to its former glory, but much to her surprise, she did. Yet another way Snowy Pine Ridge was filled with the unexpected. She'd even begun to gain new muscle tone from all of the cleaning and sanding and painting. Sure, she had an expensive membership at a boutique fitness studio in St. Louis, but the muscle tone she had gained over the past couple of weeks came with the added satisfaction of knowing she had built it through good, old-fashioned hard work.

The sky outside the windows of the mansion was dark by now, but Lacy kept on painting. She was determined to finish the dining room before she went back to the inn for the night, even if it was later than she usually stayed at the mansion. Knowing she would soon throw a massive party within its walls was an extra motivating factor, and she knew she likely had more long days like today ahead of her. She'd arrived at the mansion with the sunrise and worked steadily all day, stopping only to scarf down a quick lunch and drink some water.

But it's all starting to pay off, she thought, dipping her roller into the tray again. *The house is already so different from when I first arrived.*

And it was true. As she continued painting, her thoughts drifted through the litany of projects that she—or a contractor from town—had already accomplished. Lacy had sanded and stained the original hardwood floors, a contractor had replaced the broken windows, the plumber had made needed repairs, and Lacy had of course scrubbed and cleaned and painted until her entire body ached. And, of course, she had spent a good deal of time decluttering and staging the usable furniture. It had been even more work than she'd originally anticipated when she'd first seen the mansion, but she took enormous pride in what she had accomplished, and she had to admit to herself that she was beginning to not just admire the old mansion, but to love it.

Of course, she reminded herself, *the work is far from over... I still have an entire party to plan.*

She'd already begun making a list of things she needed to order, and she planned to source garlands, Christmas trees, and a truly staggering amount of candles the next day. That was just the beginning, though.

With everyone in town welcome to attend, she would need to make sure there was plenty of food and that the mansion looked its absolute best—both to make the party a success, but also to show everyone in Snowy Pine Ridge that it was the perfect venue. Word-of-mouth referrals were one of the best marketing tactics, and this party was an opportunity to spread the word very, very quickly about the mansion. Or, at least, she hoped it would be.

As always, doubts tried to rear their ugly heads, warning her that the party was a waste of time and money, that the mansion would never take off as a venue, and that she was making a foolish investment.

She pushed the thoughts down, dipping the roller into the paint tray with an angry vengeance and taking out her inner fears and frustrations on the dining room wall. She would be cautiously optimistic, she decided fiercely, but she would not give way to her doubts fully. Determined to think about something else, her thoughts instantly jumped to the other topic that had been circling in her mind constantly throughout the day: the locked box.

Emma, accompanied by Colette, had dropped by the inn the previous evening and given her the box. It had taken all of Lacy's willpower to maintain her self-control, accept the box with thanks, and maintain the semblance of a normal conversation until the two women had left. As soon as her bedroom door had closed behind them, however, she had dropped to the bed, shaking, as she stared at the box.

Curiosity, fear, grief, and even some excitement... so many emotions had tangled themselves up inside her as she looked at it, even though she couldn't open it yet.

What if she got her hopes up only to have them dashed and disappointed once again?

She felt equal parts the hopeful little girl she used to be and the somewhat jaded woman she had become. The vulnerability frightened her a little. Finally, she had placed it out of sight under the bed and slept fitfully, then she had woken before dawn to throw herself into work at the mansion.

A bark and then the sound of boots coming up the front steps pulled her from her once-more spiraling thoughts, and she set the paint brush down and hurried to the front door just as Derek was lifting one hand to knock. Smiling, she pulled the door open and beckoned him inside, Missy in tow.

Missy barked again, clearly only just restraining herself from throwing herself at Lacy. Her smile widening, Lacy dropped to her knees and opened her arms to welcome the fluffy puppy, who launched herself into Lacy's arms and covered her with kisses.

"Burning the midnight oil, I see," Derek commented with a crooked half-smile as he peeked into the half-painted dining room.

Lacy scooped Missy up and rose to join him in the dining room doorway. "Midnight oil? It's just past eight o'clock! I've worked far later nights back in St. Louis." She snuggled Missy closer and dropped a kiss to the puppy's furry head. "What brings you two over tonight? You know, since it's so late and all that?" she added with a teasing grin.

"Well, Missy here is a ball of energy, as we both know, and she needed an extra walk tonight to calm down enough to sleep. Besides, I was busy training one of my teams today, so she didn't get much one-on-one attention. When we were walking past and saw the lights still on, Missy begged me to stop by so she could see you."

Lacy laughed aloud at that. "So it was just 'Missy's' idea then?"

"Okay, okay, fine. It was *me* begging Missy to stop by for a visit. Are you happy now?"

"Since you admitted the truth," Lacy teased blithely, "I'm very happy, yes."

Derek rolled his eyes but he couldn't hide his grin. "Seriously, though, why are you still here working? The house will still be here in the morning."

"To be honest, I stayed late so I could distract myself."

"Distract yourself...? From what?" Realizing he might have been too forward, Derek hastily raised his hands. "Sorry, I don't mean to pry."

"No, no, you're fine. I was going to tell you anyway." Lacy took a deep breath. "Emma gave me the box Nicholas left for me."

Derek raised his eyebrows. "Really?"

Lacy nodded. "She and Colette brought it by yesterday afternoon."

"Wow... so they found it."

"Yup."

"And you have the key."

"In St. Louis, yes. I'll have to go back to get it. There's a box of my mother's things that I never went through after she passed. Maybe there's something in it that will clarify whatever I find in Nicholas's box. Not that I actually know what to expect from Nicholas's box..."

"There's only one way to find out."

Lacy sighed. "I know."

"Wow... it's going to be tough to wait to get answers."

"What do you mean?"

"Well, it's a couple of weeks until the party."

"Oh, I'm not waiting for the party to go back."

Derek blinked, looking stunned and deeply disappointed. "So you're just leaving? Just like that?"

Lacy wrinkled her brow in confusion and then realized where the miscommunication lay. Butterflies erupted in her stomach as she put the clues together and realized why he seemed so disappointed. She clenched her hand behind her back to keep from trembling and willed her voice to come out steady when she spoke. "Oh, I'm coming back for the party. I'm just going to St. Louis first."

Derek blew out a breath that he must have been holding, relief flooding his face. He blushed a little and tried to make a joke, although his eyes were still a little vulnerable.

"Good. This town would hate to lose a good party like that. Plus, we'd all miss the party planner herself."

"Just the town would miss me, huh?" She couldn't help herself. The words flew from her mouth before she could question whether it was a good idea to say them. She felt her cheeks heat up when she realized she was one hundred percent flirting with Derek, opening the door for him to flirt back.

"And me," he admitted, his voice soft. He tucked

his hands into his pockets. "I would miss you too. I've gotten used to having you around."

Their eyes caught and held, electricity buzzing between them. She swallowed, trying not to notice his freckles and the intensity in his deep brown eyes, but failing miserably. Derek took a step forward, his mouth opening as if he wanted to say something. For a brief moment, Lacy leaned toward him, as though pulled in by an unstoppable force. When their faces were just inches apart, the logical part of her brain finally caught up to her and she whirled around, breaking their gaze and picking up her paint roller again as though it was a lifeline for her to cling to.

No, she told herself fiercely, *no, you can't have him. Not with everything going on. Not when you know you'll be leaving again so soon.*

CHAPTER TWENTY

The shelf full of car cleaning kits blurred in front of Derek's eyes until his eyes only took in amorphous blobs of color, but he didn't notice. He was too lost in thought to realize that he had been standing in the same spot for a good five minutes or that he wasn't even in the correct section of the store. He had headed over to Mitchell Hardware that afternoon in a break between lessons to pick up some WD-40 and a few other things to keep up with sled maintenance. The trip, however, had proven unfruitful thus far, and he could blame it entirely on one person: Lacy Preston.

It had been all he could do not to think about her constantly, and he'd been trying to ignore the fact that he had been failing entirely in that regard. His lessons were suffering for it, and more than one client had commented on the fact that he seemed distracted. So, today, he'd made an extra effort to focus while teaching his pupils, and he'd succeeded some, but on his drive to Mitchell Hardware he had, unfortunately, passed Nicholas's old mansion and, just like that, he was pulled inexorably back to thoughts of Lacy.

"Derek!"

Derek jumped, spinning around to see his best friend, Clark, staring at him. "Clark, don't sneak up on a man like that!"

Clark folded his arms and raised an eyebrow. "You good, man? I called your name like, three or four times."

"Really?"

"Yeah. And I'm pretty sure you haven't moved in a while—I was starting to wonder if you were a cardboard cutout or something."

Derek smiled weakly at the lame joke and raked a hand through his already disheveled hair, blowing out a breath as he did so. "Guess I was just lost in thought."

Clark tilted his head, throwing Derek a knowing look. "Come on, I know you better than that. I've seen you lost in thought before, but this seems like something else."

"You know me too well."

"Well, yeah, that happens when you've been friends with someone since the second grade."

Derek gave a lopsided grin at that. "Sometimes I can't believe it's been that long."

"Stop trying to change the subject..."

"All right, all right." Derek raised his hands in surrender, knowing Clark wasn't going to be fobbed off with an excuse or by changing the subject. "Lacy is going back to St. Louis to pick a couple of things up, and she's leaving tomorrow."

Clark's eyes softened and he clapped Derek on the shoulder. "I thought this might have something to do with Lacy."

"Shut up," Derek pretended to growl, but he couldn't help laughing a little. "I know it's just for a little bit and then she'll be back for the party. I mean, the plans are well underway, so it's not like she's going to miss it after all the work she's done."

"But you're thinking about the next time she goes back to St. Louis. When she leaves for good."

Clark's words, though they were the same ones Derek had repeated to himself a million times already, still cut him like a knife to the chest. He snapped his mouth closed, merely nodding by way of a response. Clark sighed.

"I'm sorry, man. Anyone with eyes in this town can see that there's something between the two of you."

Derek blinked, rearing his head back a little. "Are people talking?"

"If they are, what do you care?"

Derek shrugged. "I guess you're right..."

"And that's not really what's bothering you anyway. It really all comes down to what you're going to do when Lacy leaves for good, doesn't it?"

Derek shot Clark a look. "You run a hardware store. Since when did you become so perceptive? I feel like I'm in therapy or something."

Clark laughed. "You know how people spill their deepest secrets to bartenders? Well, folks tell me a lot more than you'd think when I'm checking them out at the cash register."

"Is that so? Wow, I bet you have juicy stories to tell."

"Stop trying to change the subject!"

Before Derek could reply, they had to step aside to make room for an elderly customer pushing his cart to pass by. The man paused, realizing who was standing and talking to Clark, and his face lit up.

"Young man, I heard all about the Christmas party your girlfriend is putting on at the Spielman mansion! I have to say, I'm pleased as punch to see the old house gettin' all fixed up. Your young lady is stayin' true to Nicholas's memory, God rest his soul, and all of us in town are right glad to see it." The man reached one wrinkled hand out to shake Derek's.

Derek, overwhelmed by the onslaught of the man's speech, struggled to keep up. "Oh, Lacy isn't my girlfriend—"

"Well, whatever you youngsters call it today," the man said, waving Derek's protest aside. "Me and my wife are lookin' forward to the Christmas party, I can tell you that."

Out of the corner of his eye, Derek could see that Clark was struggling to hold back a peal of laughter. Derek shot him a venomous look then turned back to the elderly customer.

"Well... I'll be sure to pass your compliments along," Derek finally said, his voice weak.

"You do that, son. You do that."

The man continued pushing his cart and disappeared down the aisle. When he was out of earshot, Clark finally gave in to his suppressed hilarity. Derek gave him a playful slug on the arm.

"Come on, man! Pull yourself together."

"Sorry, sorry." Clark wiped at his streaming eyes. "Phew, I needed that today."

"So glad my discomfort is a source of pleasure for you," Derek replied, his tone dry.

Clark sobered then, his face becoming serious. "It's really not. Mervin always cracks me up. He comes in a lot. No, what you're going through right now with Lacy doesn't make me laugh. I'm worried about you."

Derek sighed, his defenses coming down before Clark's kindly gaze.

"What should I do? I think I'm falling for her," he admitted, and he realized how true it was as the words left his mouth. He hadn't spoken them aloud to anyone, almost too afraid to admit it even to himself, but there was no denying it any longer. "I'm falling for her, and it's the dumbest thing I could've done. I mean, she's leaving."

Clark chewed the inside of his cheek. "Have you told Lacy how you feel?"

Derek shook his head. "We hardly know each other. Do you know how crazy that would sound?"

"People can fall in love at first sight."

Derek wrinkled his forehead. "That's from movies and books. Not real life. Besides, I didn't fall in love at first sight." Although, even as he said it, his mind flew back to that first night he'd met her, when she'd been illuminated by the lamp on his sled, and she'd flown at him in such a rage for scaring her. He'd felt something inside him shift even at that moment. It may not have been love, but it *had* been a spark.

Clark sighed, rolling his eyes. "That's not what I mean—I was trying to say that people can fall in love quickly. Just because you haven't known Lacy long doesn't make your feelings for her any less real." He paused. "I think you should tell her."

"Why? What would be the point?"

"She deserves to know. How can you just let her walk away without telling her? Are you really going to let this chance slip through your fingers?"

Derek pulled in a breath, considering Clark's words. Finally, he exhaled and, as he did so, he acknowledged the truth of what his friend had said. "You're right," he admitted, his voice soft.

"I know I'm right," Clark replied, laughing a little. "What are you still standing around talking to me for? Go get your girl, Derek!"

Rolling his eyes and laughing as well, Derek clapped Clark on the shoulder and hurried out of the store, pulling his phone from his pocket as he did so. In his truck, he listened as Lacy's line rang, his heart pounding. This would be their official first date, if she said yes. And he really, really hoped she would say yes.

After three rings, she picked up. "Hey, Derek. What's up?"

"Hi." His voice sounded a little too breathless, so he paused and told himself fiercely to pull it together. "I know you're leaving tomorrow, but I was wondering if you'd like to have dinner tonight. With me."

Lacy paused, and he thought his heart might beat out of his chest. "Okay," she said, her voice warm, the way it sounded when she smiled. "When and where?"

Relief flooded through Derek. "Bella Notte, six o'clock? It's a nice Italian place, best in town. I think you'll love it."

"Hey, I trust your judgment," Lacy said with a chuckle. "You know this town backwards and forwards. Okay, I'll meet you there?"

"Remember how I said my mother raised me right? I'll pick you up at the inn."

"Sounds good. See you then."

Derek said goodbye, then they ended the call. He tipped his head back against the seat, his adrenaline still racing. She had said yes to the date, and that meant no more excuses—he vowed then and there that he would take Clark's advice and tell Lacy about his feelings that night at Bella Notte.

* * *

"He's taking you *tonight*?" Madeline's voice was nearly a screech through the phone. "Girl, what has he been waiting for? Doesn't he know you're leaving in the morning?"

"He knows," Lacy replied, folding a couple of outfits for her whirlwind trip back to St. Louis and packing them into her carry-on suitcase. "But, Mads, I'm pretty sure this is an actual date. He's picking me up and he's taking me to the nicest place in town."

Madeline gave a low whistle over the phone. "So romantic! Actually, now that I think about it, maybe he picked tonight because he had to stake his claim before you leave town."

Lacy rolled her eyes at that. "Come on, Madeline. What kind of men are you dating that you would think that?"

"Um... maybe because I went out with a stockbroker last weekend who took me to a club and spent the night flirting with other women but when I tried to talk to anyone else he got super jealous."

"Gross."

"Tell me about it." Madeline pushed and, when she spoke again, her voice was softer. "Seriously, are you doing okay? I mean, with the box and the mansion and... and everything."

Lacy blew out a sigh and stopped packing for a moment, turning to sink onto the mattress. "I don't know, honestly. My thoughts and emotions have been a swirling mess for days. I have no clue what might be in that box and coming to terms with the fact that my mom may have lied to me my whole life about my father and grandfather? It's... a lot to deal with."

"And then there's Derek."

"And then there's Derek," Lacy agreed, rubbing her free hand across her eyes. "He came out of nowhere and... Mads, it's ridiculous to have feelings for a guy I just met. I mean, it would never work! I'm going back to St. Louis and we both know long distance relationships never last."

"Yeah, well, I'm living proof that in-person relationships don't always last either. The dating scene here in St. Louis is *rough*, girl."

Lacy pulled a face, laughing a little. "Okay, you might be right about that. It's just... I had no idea I would meet Derek, but things with him have been so easy ever since we met. We became friends almost instantly, and my feelings for him have just grown from there." Lacy sat up, clutching the phone to her ear. "Madeline," she said softly, "I really, *really* like him."

"So get out of your own way," Madeline responded, but her voice was gentle.

"I'm trying, I promise."

"And," Madeline continued, playful now. "Make sure you're dressed to kill tonight. FaceTime me so we can pick an outfit."

"Right now?"

"Right now. Isn't he coming in like twenty minutes?"

Lacy glanced at her watch and gasped. "Oh my gosh, yes. I need to pick an outfit, stat!"

Lacy clicked the button to FaceTime and for the next five minutes the two of them sorted through Lacy's meager supply of clothes to pick an outfit for the date. Finally, after much deliberation, they settled on an elegant and stylish black jumpsuit with heeled booties and simple jewelry. It was one of Lacy's favorite outfits, one that she knew flattered her and looked dressy without being pretentious.

"You look stunning," Madeline assured her after Lacy had put it on.

"Are you sure? I want to look perfect."

"You do." Madeline laughed. "And see? This is further proof that you like him. I've helped you get ready for dates before where you opted not to even change out of your work clothes. You actually *care* tonight. You really do like this guy."

Lacy paused, not sure how to answer that. Luckily, a knock on her door saved her from acknowledging the truth of Madeline's words. "I have to get that."

"Good luck!"

"Thanks. Night!"

Lacy hung up, her pulse racing. Smoothing her hair and taking one last glance in the mirror, Lacy walked to the door.

CHAPTER TWENTY-ONE

It was all Derek could do not to gasp aloud when Lacy opened the door. As it was, he only just managed to keep his mouth from gaping open, although he was pretty sure his eyes had widened enough to give away just how much she had taken his breath away. She looked absolutely stunning, like she had stepped from the pages of a New York fashion runway. Derek didn't know much about fashion, but he definitely noticed the way the jumpsuit cinched at her waist, highlighting how petite it was and showing off her delicate hourglass figure. Her hair was loosely curled, brushing the tips of her shoulders and her eyes arrested him, lashes seeming to go on for miles. She had clearly made an effort, and it hit him once more with full force that this was a real date.

"You look... you look..." Derek could have cursed himself for how foolish and tongue-tied he sounded, like a schoolboy trying to talk to a girl for the first time.

"That bad?" she teased.

Derek felt his cheeks warm even as he laughed, breaking the tension somewhat. "I was going to say that you look beautiful."

Now it was Lacy's turn to blush ever so slightly, her cheeks pinking up so adorably that he had to keep himself from pulling her into his arms right then and there.

Keep it together, man, he told himself. *This is your first date. Oh, and she's leaving.*

Lacy tucked her hair behind one ear, revealing an elegant and simple silver earring.

"You clean up pretty good too, Morse," Lacy said, keeping her tone light, but the way she was looking at him told him she wasn't feeling quite as casually about him as she was pretending.

"I showered and everything."

Lacy pretended to sniff. "Oh, good, that means I can breathe freely tonight. Derek, you treat me like a princess. I'm honored."

"Breathe away, your highness," he replied, sweeping a low bow that set her off, her delightful laughter filling the air, much to his pleasure. "Your carriage awaits, at your leisure."

"Excellent. I hope it's not far, because I'm starving, and you have about fifteen minutes before I become an entirely different person," Lacy joked.

Derek pretended to look afraid. "In that case, we have no time to waste."

Without warning, he grabbed her around the waist and threw her over his shoulder like a sack of potatoes and began carrying her down the hallway and into the lobby of the inn. Lacy squealed with surprise.

"What are you doing?" She could barely get the words out around her laughter. "People are looking at us!"

"Let 'em look." He was grinning from ear to ear and he made sure to give the girl working the front desk a polite nod, pretending that it was completely normal to carry a woman over his shoulder.

"Derek!"

"All right, all right," Derek conceded.

He swung her off his shoulder and into a cradled position in his arms, about to set her down on the snowy sidewalk when Lacy paused, resting in his arms. "What?"

"Well... the snow. Maybe you can hold me a little longer, at least until we get to your truck," she said, looking up at him with twinkling mischief in her eyes.

Derek rolled his. "So *now* you want to be carried. At your service, my queen."

Lacy gave him a regal nod that made him laugh and he began carrying her across the snow-piled parking lot. Soon enough he had her settled on the passenger seat of his truck. They talked and listened to oldies while they drove to Bella Notte, and he discovered that she loved Etta James and Frank Sinatra just as much as he did. She was just telling him about why she'd never been able to get into Bing Crosby when they pulled up to the restaurant.

"Wow, this looks like a really nice place," she commented, taking it in.

"I know it's probably nothing compared to the places you go in St. Louis—"

"Hey," she said, cutting him off and laying her hand on his arm. "Don't sell Snowy Pine Ridge, or yourself, short. This looks beautiful."

Derek smiled. "Wait until you see inside."

When they walked through the double doors of

Bella Notte and Derek had given his name, the host walked them through the intimate dining room to a cozy booth at the back. Lacy looked around as she slid into the booth, and Derek hoped she liked what she saw. White tablecloths covered the tables that dotted the checkerboard floor and candles burned on each one, emitting a soft glow. A man in a tuxedo played quiet dinner music on a grand piano in one corner of the large room. Everything about Bella Notte felt at once intimate and elegant.

"This is really nice."

"I'm glad you like it. You know, I actually brought my first ever date here, all the way back in high school."

Lacy raised her eyebrows and glanced over the menu, her eyes widening. "Really? Seems like kind of a steep price tag for a high schooler."

Derek laughed. "Oh, it was, trust me. I had no idea what I was doing and I thought going on a date meant spending a fortune every time. Blame it on all the old romantic movies I used to watch with my mom." Derek shot her a look. "And don't tease me for watching old romantic movies with my mom."

Lacy laughed. "I wasn't going to!"

"Oh, yes you were. I saw it in your eyes."

"No, I wasn't!" Lacy protested. "I think it's sweet

that you spent time with your mom when you were a teen. Not many do, and I'm sure she loved it."

Derek shrugged. "I think she did. As for my dating life, I still feel like I don't know what I'm doing even now."

"Hey, I get it. I feel that way sometimes too. The dating scene is rough in St. Louis. For the record, though, I think you're doing a great job," she said, giving him a little wink that made him grin.

A waiter came to the table then, asking if they wanted anything to drink. Lacy ordered a water and Derek asked for one as well, adding that he'd like a bottle of wine for the table. The waiter launched into a litany of the wines available and Derek panicked a little, ultimately choosing the first one the waiter said that he recognized.

This is just what I was telling Lacy, he thought as the waiter walked away, *I have no idea what I'm doing.*

"That's my favorite wine," Lacy commented.

Relief flooded through Derek. "That's why I picked it."

"Oh, come on." Lacy laughed. "You had no idea when you picked it."

"Maybe. Maybe not. I'll never tell." He wiggled his eyebrows at her, making her laugh again.

Derek loved this, loved the easy way they could talk to each other, even when he felt a little out of his element. Being with her felt natural, and she never failed to lighten his spirits and make him laugh. Lacy toyed with her napkin and studied him.

"Derek," she began, her voice a little hesitant now. "When we were talking about dating before, it made me wonder—have you ever found someone you were really serious about?"

Derek sat back in his chair, thinking about her question. It didn't bother him that she'd asked. In fact, he'd been wondering the same thing about her.

"I've been in a couple of longish relationships, but they never got too serious, no."

"Same for me," Lacy admitted, but she looked a little troubled.

Does she think I could never be serious with someone? he wondered. *Does she think I never want to settle down?*

If he was honest with himself, he'd asked himself the same questions before. He'd just never seemed to find someone with whom he'd really found a lasting connection, and over the years he'd begun to wonder if he just wasn't cut out for marriage, if he was just missing some vital component that led to lasting relationships.

Looking at Lacy across the table, though, he felt something stirring within himself that he'd never felt before. It made no sense—she was only here temporarily, after all—but when he looked into her eyes he could envision the kind of love that led to settling down.

Their gaze caught and held and he felt the spark swirling in the air between them.

"Lacy," he began, not even sure what he wanted to say, but feeling it was finally time to tell her how he felt. "I—"

Before he could finish, the waiter came back with their drinks, giving them a friendly smile and a nod. Derek broke off, clearing his throat as the moment slipped away.

* * *

Lacy forced herself to look down at her menu while the waiter poured out their glasses of wine, her heart racing. There had been something in Derek's eyes just then when he'd looked at her, something about the expression on his face that had made her pulse speed up. The way he'd looked at her... it had been so serious, so tender, that it had made her heart ache.

Was he feeling the same way she was?

Because the truth was, even though it made no sense, she couldn't hide from the fact that she wanted to be with Derek any longer. Admitting that to herself frightened her enough that she consumed herself with the menu, focusing on it with a determination that was hardly warranted when picking an entree.

"See anything you like?" Derek asked, studying his own menu.

Lacy blinked, confused for a moment and then blushed when she realized he meant the menu options and not himself.

"Um..." She reread the menu items, the descriptions finally getting through her muddled brain and beginning to make sense. As she read, the foodie side of her came out and she realized the food *did* sound incredible. "Ooh, I think I want to try the chicken cacciatore."

"I haven't had that one yet! Their eggplant parmesan and spaghetti Bolognese are incredible. If you get the chicken cacciatore and I get something you like, want to try each other's?"

"I thought you'd never ask," Lacy teased. "I had my eye on the salmon piccata, as well."

"That sounds amazing too. How about I get that?"

"Sounds good to me!"

Derek turned to the waiter, who was waiting for their final orders.

"We'll get a caprese salad and some bruschetta to start," Derek told the waiter, who nodded ceremoniously. "And I'll have the salmon piccata with the lemon garlic rigatoni. Lacy?"

"And I'll have the chicken cacciatore."

The waiter glided away, leaving them alone once more. Lacy had been pleasantly surprised to discover that Derek was a foodie like her—for some reason, she'd just assumed a guy from a small town would be into burgers and beers, but he was knowledgeable about the menu at a place like Bella Notte, which told her a lot. She took a sip of her water, trying not to notice how close their legs were beneath the table, or the way his strong and calloused hand rested on the white tablecloth and the way she wanted that hand to hold hers.

"How's the house coming?"

Lacy pulled herself back to the present, pushing her twitterpated thoughts aside. "It's nearly finished!" She pulled a face. "Well, with a house like that, it will never be 'finished' since there's always more that could be done, but it's really coming along. I think by the Christmas party it's going to be in shining condition. Speaking of, I can't wait for you to see the decorations I've picked out!" Lacy leaned forward, getting excited now. "In addition to the enormous tree for the front parlor and the garlands for the fireplaces and the staircase, I'm getting about a million twinkle lights, tons of candles, and lots of poinsettias. Picture a scene from a snow globe, basically."

"That sounds gorgeous. Do you need help?"

"You bet I'll need help," Lacy said with a laugh. "Hanging all the lights alone is going to be a job and a half."

"Count me in. Derek Morse, at your service."

Lacy smiled. "Thanks. I knew I could count on you."

"Oh, I see. So that's why you said yes to this date. You're wining and dining me to get me to work for you."

"Busted!" she said with a laugh.

He sighed dramatically. "Well, at least you bought me dinner first."

She wiggled her eyebrows. "What is it you always say? 'I was raised right'?"

"Exactly." He nodded, grinning. "I know how to treat my dates."

Their banter continued over the next few

minutes, making Lacy's heart swell with contented enjoyment. She loved the way they could talk about serious things or about absolutely nothing and that both were easy with him. This was so unlike many of the dates she'd gone on back home—stilted conversation, awkwardly picking at their food, trying to figure out if there should be a kiss at the end or not. No, with Derek, it was just... natural.

The waiter arrived with their food, setting the gorgeous plates in front of them and slipped away once again, but not before refilling their wine glasses. Lacy wiggled in her seat, leaning forward to breathe in the heady aromas of the dishes. Derek lifted the plate of bruschetta toward her, offering her a piece. She bit into the crusty bread, savoring the fresh flavors as they danced across her palate and covering her mouth with one hand.

"Heaven," she murmured around the bite.

"Amen," Derek agreed, looking into her eyes, even though Lacy noticed he hadn't taken a bite yet, too busy looking at her.

Lacy took another bite, contentment spreading through her. Though it made no sense, her meeting Derek on this trip to Snowy Pine Ridge that she had thought was an interruption to her real life in St. Louis, she felt at that moment that she was exactly where she needed to be. The feeling surprised her and she sat back, savoring the moment and looking into Derek's eyes.

She didn't know where this thing between them was heading, but she did know one thing. She was glad she was taking that leap of faith with Derek by her side.

CHAPTER TWENTY-TWO

As they left Bella Notte, Derek already knew he didn't want the night to end just yet. It didn't take long for him to think up a solution and he pitched his idea as Lacy was buckling her seat belt in the truck.

"What do you say we drive over to Main Street and walk along the main drag? The Christmas lights look amazing at night, and they play Christmas music over the outdoor speakers."

"I think that sounds perfect." Lacy patted her stomach. "You might have to roll me down Main Street after all that food, but I'm game."

"Good." Derek put the truck in gear and headed out of the parking lot. "You're in town at just the right time of year. This is when Snowy Pine Ridge really shines."

"If you're giving me a sales pitch, I'll stop you there—I actually already love it here."

"Really?"

"Don't look so surprised. It's like a scene out of *White Christmas*. What's not to love?"

Derek tried not to get his hopes up at her casual words. *It doesn't mean she wants to stay,* he reminded himself.

As they drove, Derek thought he caught Lacy humming along quietly with "Have Yourself A Merry Little Christmas" on the radio, and it made him smile. She'd opened up and relaxed so much since he'd first met her, and he loved seeing all of the new sides of her that loved fun and spontaneity. He glanced over at her as he parked the truck on Main Street, marveling again at how beautiful she looked and that she'd said yes to this date. Lacy looked over, caught him staring, and raised an eyebrow.

"Do I have food on my face or something?" she teased. "Because, if so, a gentleman would've told me back at the restaurant."

"You have an entire ravioli stuck to the side of your lip, yes," he joked back.

Lacy rolled her eyes even as she laughed. "We didn't even order ravioli."

"Incredible how you still managed to get one all over your face then."

Lacy stuck out her tongue. "Keep this up and you won't get a goodnight kiss."

Derek's heart stopped at her playful words and it was all he could do to keep his breathing even. "In that case, I take it all back."

"Smart man."

"I may not be the brightest, but that one is a no-brainer," he agreed soulfully, making her laugh again.

Derek hurried around the truck to open the door for Lacy and helped her down from the giant step. As they began walking down the street, admiring the lights and the general holiday ambiance, Derek itched to hold her hand. She'd teased him about kissing him goodnight, but he didn't know if she was actually serious or not, and, as they continued to walk, panic about the fact that he still hadn't told her how he felt began to set in. It was all well and good to banter like they always did, but she deserved to know that his feelings for her were real, not another shared joke between them. Lost in his own thoughts, he didn't even realize they'd been walking for quite some time or that Lacy had been trying to talk to him until she stopped walking abruptly.

"Are you listening to me?" Lacy was grinning as

she waved a hand in front of his face and he blinked. "Hello? Anybody home?"

"Sorry, er... I guess I was lost in my own thoughts."

Lacy's smile dropped away as she studied his face, her eyes searching his now. "Is something wrong?"

Derek mustered up a smile but even he could tell it probably didn't look genuine. "Why would something be wrong? I'm with the one and only Lacy Preston tonight."

"Hey, I'm being serious," she chided gently. "You looked so..." She trailed off, and it was her turn to look a little embarrassed.

"A little what?"

"I don't know, there was a sadness in your eyes," Lacy finally said, then quickly waved a hand as though to swipe her words away. "Don't listen to me, I'm probably just reading into things."

Derek caught her hand then, unable to help himself, stilling her movement. "You're not reading into things," he admitted, his voice lower then. "I keep thinking about the fact that you're going back to St. Louis in the morning."

Lacy's eyes softened and she threaded her fingers through his. "You know I'm coming back, though."

"I know."

"So...?"

Derek almost spilled the truth right then and there but, as he opened his mouth to tell her how he felt, it was as though his throat closed off, leaving him unable to speak. He hesitated, his mind swirling.

Just tell her. Now is the time, one part of his mind screamed.

The other side of him, however, voted for caution. What if he told her how serious his feelings for her were and it scared her off?

He couldn't very well come out and say, "Hey, Lacy, don't move back to St. Louis. I want you to stay in Snowy Pine Ridge. Forever. With me." That was unlikely to go over well. It was too much, too soon, and he knew it, even if he also knew that what he felt for her was the real thing.

"So there are things we still need to do before you leave," Derek said, an idea coming to him and giving him an out for the moment.

Lacy laughed. "Okay, I'll bite. What things?"

"Well, for starters, we haven't been ice skating yet and you specifically said you wanted to."

"I'm pretty sure I said that to get out of dogsledding."

"I'm serious," Derek protested, and he realized in

that moment just how serious he was about it. All he knew was that he couldn't let the date end, not yet, not when he hadn't found the courage to open up to her. "You've got to go ice skating before you leave."

Lacy cocked her head to the side, her brow wrinkling a little. "You are serious, aren't you?"

"Of course I am! Come on, the ice rink is only a few more blocks down the street."

Laughing a little, Lacy gave in. "I see I have no choice in the matter, Mr. Morse. Lead the way."

"That's the spirit," he teased back, tugging her hand playfully as they began walking again.

Up ahead, Happy Glacier Rink hulked on the corner ahead, its paint peeling and all the lights off. It was a gloomy looking building on the best of days, but the darkness did nothing to make up for its lack of charm. Lacy paused in front of it, pursing her lips.

"Not to be a wet blanket, but the rink looks very much... closed," Lacy said.

Derek wiggled his eyebrows. "Good thing I know a way in."

"A way in... Derek Morse, are you talking about breaking and entering??"

"Nothing like that," he assured her with a grin. "Think of it like... creatively choosing our own hours, even when the rink isn't technically open."

"Well, when you put it like that..." Lacy rolled her eyes, but she was smiling now too. "What about the owner? Randy? Randolph? What was his name?"

"Rudolph."

Lacy choked back a laugh at the name. "Right, Rudolph. Didn't you tell me he's an insanely grumpy old man? What if he catches us?"

"Well, his house *is* right next to the rink," Derek told her cheerfully, enjoying her dismay as her eyes popped wide open. "But seriously, it'll be fine. The secret way is on the side furthest from his house and we'll skate by moonlight. He'll never know we were there."

"I don't know..."

"Come on, Preston, you've got to live it up before you're back in the boring city. No place knows how to party like a small town." When that wasn't working, he gave her one last tease. "Or are you chicken?"

Lacy narrowed her eyes and smirked. "Never. Lead the way, Morse."

Taking her hand once more, Derek led the way down the narrow alley that snaked behind the rink, leading her to a rusty old door that sat beside the dumpster. He turned the handle, jiggled it a little, then yanked up hard as he pulled back. With a groan, the door gave way and opened. Derek glanced at Lacy, pleased to see her eyes widen in surprise, as though she hadn't really believed he could get them into the rink. He'd had plenty of experience sneaking into the rink and had perfected the steps to open the rusty door over the years.

Once inside, Derek led her through the dim interior to the skate rental booth and they helped themselves to skates. Whispering and laughing quietly, the two took off their shoes and laced on their skates, hobbling over to the waiting ice. Moonlight from a few small skylights overhead guided them as they pushed off onto the ice. Immediately, Lacy began windmilling to keep her balance, her feet sliding in opposite directions. Holding back a laugh, Derek extended his arm for support just in time. Lacy grabbed onto it, only just staying upright.

"It's been a while since I skated," Lacy said with a laugh.

"Has it? I never would've guessed," Derek replied innocently, which set Lacy off again, her tinkling laugh filling the quiet rink.

Holding her hand, Derek guided Lacy around the rink. Soon enough, she found her rhythm and began skating with less shakiness. When he deemed her safe enough to skate alone, Derek skated backward ahead of her.

"I dare you to race me," he challenged, cocking an eyebrow.

"What are we, eleven?"

"Quit stalling, Preston."

"Oh, you're on. First one to the other wall wins."

Derek skated so he was beside her. "On your mark, get set..."

"Go!" Lacy shouted, already skating before the words had left her lips.

"Cheater!" Derek called, barely able to speak through his laughter.

He pushed off to catch up to her as she blazed erratically forward. He reached for her swinging arms and grabbed one of them to pull her back, but he lost his balance just as he caught hold of her. His skates slid out from under him and he wrapped his arms around her to cushion their fall just in time, twisting as he fell so that she landed on top of him instead of on the ice. For a moment, the wind was knocked out of him, but he stopped being aware of that almost immediately. Instead, he was keenly aware of Lacy laying in his arms, her face only inches from his.

Electricity sizzled between them and that

magnetism that always pulled them together returned in full force. Without taking the time to think about whether it was a good idea or not, Derek lifted one hand to cup the nape of her neck, feeling as though he were pulled by a force stronger than his own will. Her lips, soft and beautiful, parted slightly as her eyes fluttered closed and she bridged the gap between them until her lips brushed his. Derek kissed her back, savoring the sweetness of the kiss.

Suddenly, a blinding spotlight landed on them, making them break apart in confusion. "What are you doing in my rink?" a grumpy voice hollered.

"Come on!" Derek cried, pulling Lacy to her feet.

They scrambled off the ice, untying their skates as Rudolph ran toward them. In stocking feet, they simply grabbed their shoes and raced toward the back door, hearing his slower footfalls thudding behind them. Outside, Derek picked Lacy up so she wouldn't have to run in the snow and sprinted down the sidewalk. Rudolph slowed, too old and tired to keep up with them. A few blocks later they lost him, and Derek collapsed into a snowbank, relinquishing his hold on Lacy. The two flopped in the snow, laughing until their sides ached at their narrow escape.

Derek rolled to his side to look at Lacy, breathing in the sight of her hair laying in the snow all wild and free, her head tipped back as she laughed. It was just about the most beautiful thing he'd ever seen, and it made all the hilarity evaporate from him in an instant. One hand on her cheek, he lowered his head and kissed her softly one last time, but this time felt more final. When they broke apart, he rested his head on her forehead for a few moments, searching inside for the joy they'd been swept away in only minutes before. It still lingered there, but it mingled with the bittersweet knowledge that Lacy would be leaving in the morning. And then again, this time for good, after the Christmas party.

CHAPTER TWENTY-THREE

Lacy had thought she would be glad to arrive back at her St. Louis apartment, but as she walked inside she felt nothing but a sense of loneliness. It felt dark and lonely after her cozy room at the inn and, although it was tastefully decorated, it felt rather soulless and aloof to her now. She dropped her keys into the bowl that rested on the credenza in the foyer, looking around and rubbing her upper arms as though chilled, even though the apartment was warm. "Home, sweet home," she murmured, and her voice sounded too loud in the utter stillness enveloping her.

Shrugging off her coat and pushing her suitcase to the side with one foot, she decided then and there to jump into the task awaiting her. Chest tight, she hurried to her bedroom and dug through her stash of jewelry. There, buried beneath accessories she hadn't worn in years, rested the old key necklace from her grandfather. She disentangled it from another necklace, picking at the knot in the chain until the two slid apart and held it in the palm of her hand almost reverently, studying the delicate swirls in the metalwork on the key. It had a reassuring weight as it rested in her hand, and she felt the tension in her chest ease ever so slightly. Even though the box was still back in Snowy Pine Ridge, she decided on a whim to put the necklace on once more, clasping it behind her neck and letting it settle to rest by her heart beneath her blouse.

Feeling a little stronger now, she pulled in a deep breath. It was time for the next task—looking through the box of her mother's leftover things. Making her way to her storage closet, she grunted as she pushed aside heavy boxes until she found the one she was looking for. She blew off a layer of dust before picking it up, and the dust cloud made her sneeze. Once again, the sound was startlingly loud in her silent apartment, and she keenly felt the loss of the people she'd become close to in Snowy Pine Ridge. Especially Derek.

Memories of their date and the kiss at the end

of it made her cheeks warm and she pressed her hands to her cheeks until they cooled beneath her fingers once more. That kiss had been more than breathtaking, but even more than the attraction she felt toward Derek, she simply missed his friendship.

I wish he was here right now, she realized. *I wish he was here to hold my hand and sit beside me so I didn't have to do this alone.*

He would know the right things to say and he would know how to bring a smile to her face even amidst all of the emotions that looking through her mother's things would bring to the surface. She debated calling him for a moment, but she shoved the thought aside. This was something she needed to do alone.

Carrying the box into her living room, she sat down on the floor in front of the couch and lifted the dusty lid. Mounds of disorganized papers and various mementos were stuffed into the box at random, and Lacy began digging through the box to sort through its tumbled contents.

As she pulled out a stack of old tax documents, Lacy gasped as piles of unopened letters came into view. With trembling fingers, she set the tax papers aside, reaching for the top envelope. To her horror, it was addressed to her. The return address bore the name Nicholas Spielman.

Her breathing now coming in broken gasps, Lacy pawed through the box and discovered letter after unopened letter from her father and grandfather. Pain, grief, anger, and a myriad of other emotions crashed over her, stealing her breath and slicing through her heart. She dropped the letters, covering her eyes with her hands as huge, gasping sobs began to rack her body. She curled into herself tightly, rocking slightly as scalding hot tears welled in her eyes and squeezed between the fingers she still pressed to her face.

"All these years," she moaned aloud. "All these years, and I never knew."

Lacy lay curled up on the floor, unable to do anything but weep. An unexpected anger against her mother forced itself upon her and she began to cry even harder. How could her mother have lied to her for so many years? Have kept those letters from her own daughter? Lacy had been heartbroken when her father had left them—or at least, she had thought he had left them, but now she knew that was a lie. She had built her whole life around trying to distance herself from Harv and Nicholas, working herself to the brink of exhaustion and back, and all of it had been because of a lie. She had missed out on years of a relationship with a parent and a grandparent who loved her, and for what? For absolutely nothing, and now it was forever too late to rebuild the bridges her mother had burned from sheer pettiness.

She wasn't sure how long she had been laying on the floor when the violence of her tears finally began to subside. With a hiccup, her eyes swollen and aching, she slowly pushed herself up to a sitting position and looked down at the stack of letters all addressed to her. Each of them a physical representation of love for a little girl who had not been abandoned, but had been forcibly kept from a relationship with those who cared for her. She knew that reading the letters would provoke another storm of emotions and, though she longed to read them, she knew that she needed to give herself some time to prepare.

Pulling herself to her feet, she walked to the foyer to grab her phone from her purse. She needed someone to talk to right that minute, and she knew that she couldn't handle being alone any longer, not when the pain was still so fresh. Fishing the phone from an inner purse pocket, she dialed Madeline's number. To her relief, her friend picked up on the second ring.

"Lacy! Calling to tell me some juicy gossip about your date with the hot lumberjack?"

In spite of herself, Madeline's boisterous greeting brought a smile to her lips. It was the feeble ghost of a smile, but it was still something. "Not exactly... Madeline, I just found out that my mother lied to me about my dad and Nicholas. They didn't abandon me."

Madeline's gasp crackled over the line. "What? Lacy, oh my gosh, are you serious?"

"I wish I was kidding. I was just looking through the box of papers I never sorted through after Mom passed. There are stacks on stacks of unopened letters they wrote to me."

"Oh, Lacy..."

Lacy slumped onto the couch. "I know."

"I can't even imagine what you're going through right now."

"Believe me, I wish I wasn't going through it."

"If I could take it from you, I would."

"I know, Mads. That's why I love you."

"Well, you shouldn't be alone at a time like this. I'm dropping work and taking you out for a late lunch. Let's meet at Basil & Sage in twenty minutes. Does that work for you?"

Lacy sat up straighter, brushing away fresh tears.

She knew how busy Madeline was with work, and the fact that Madeline would just drop everything to spend time with her meant the world. Basil & Sage was their favorite bistro, and they'd spent countless hours chatting and catching up within its elegant and relaxing walls.

"Are you sure? I know you've got a lot on your plate," Lacy hedged, although every part of her hoped Madeline wouldn't back out.

"You're more important than what I have going at work today. Don't fight me on this, okay? Just get over to the bistro."

"Yes, ma'am," Lacy replied, giving a watery laugh. Love and gratitude for her friend washed over her. "Thanks, Madeline. I don't know what I'd do without you."

Twenty minutes later, Lacy had freshened up and was walking through the giant double doors of the bistro. Madeline was waiting at their usual table and she stood as she saw Lacy enter, hurrying over to wrap her in a tight hug. Madeline's signature perfume met Lacy as she hugged her friend back, and she felt some of the pain that had held her in a death grip easing up some now that she was in the presence of her best friend.

"I hope you don't mind," Madeline said as they

settled themselves at their table, "but I ordered for us already. I thought you wouldn't want to worry about picking through the menu."

"Thanks." Lacy rested against the back of her chair, exhausted to her very bones. "I don't think I would've been capable of making one more decision today. What'd you pick?"

"Bacon-wrapped feta-stuffed figs, a Greek salad, and a flatbread with olives, hummus, and shaved lamb."

"You know, I didn't think I could eat when you mentioned lunch, but just hearing that I think I'm suddenly starving."

It was a lame joke, but Madeline smiled at her anyway. "Okay, tell me everything."

That was all it took. As the waiter brought out their food and refilled their glasses of water with lemon wedges, Lacy told Madeline all that was crowding her heart and mind, starting with the letters.

"I feel like my whole world has been tilted, Mads. Everything I thought I knew about them was a lie, and now I have to come to terms with that."

"I can't even imagine going through a shift in worldview like that."

"It's crazy hard. So many things I thought were

one way turned out not to be true. I could've had a relationship with them, both of them, Madeline. I could've had a dad and a grandpa in my life, and instead I grew up believing I'd been unloved and abandoned. They clearly wanted to be in my life, and they must have wondered why I never wrote back."

"You can't blame yourself for that part. You had no idea."

"I know, but it still hurts to know what we could've had and what will never be now. It's too late."

Madeline reached out and squeezed Lacy's hand, her eyes soft. "I'm so sorry."

"I mean, everything I've done in my life—like my career—was to prove that I'm *not* like them. Without that motivating me, what do I have left?"

"You still have a successful career," Madeline pointed out, taking a bite of a stuffed fig.

"I know, but..." Lacy looked down at her hands, her fingers twisted together in her lap. "I'm not sure it's what I want anymore." She snapped her mouth shut, finally looking up at Madeline to gauge her friend's reaction. She hadn't even admitted the truth to herself yet, but she'd said the words aloud now and she knew they were true.

"Wow. So what does that mean for you? What do you really want?"

"I'm not sure. I just... I don't know if I'm happy here. But if I walk away, what do I have left? After all that work, it feels like giving up."

"I wouldn't look at it that way." Madeline took a thoughtful sip of her water. "Changing course doesn't necessarily mean you're giving up or that you've lost your way. Sometimes it means you're forging a new path, finding a new dream that actually makes you happy."

Lacy's heart eased up at Madeline's words. She hadn't expected her career-driven friend to see it that way. "Do you really think so?"

"I really do. Life is too short, as you're well aware."

Lacy murmured an agreement. She'd been learning that all too well over the course of that harrowing day.

"So, what now?" Madeline asked again. "I know you're heartbroken today, but there's something different about you now. I noticed it as soon as I saw you again. You hold yourself differently and there's a lightness behind all of the sorrow you're carrying today. I think Snowy Pine Ridge has been good for you."

Lacy took a bite of her flatbread, chewing it thoughtfully. "I think you're right," she finally admitted. "Being there... I think it's changed me."

"And for the better. I think you should pursue that happiness. Pursue whatever put that lightness into your eyes."

Lacy toyed with her napkin. She knew Madeline was right, and yet... "Madeline, I don't know if I'm brave enough. I mean, it would be an entire life shift. That's a big deal."

"It is, but, Lacy, I think it could be worth it. You *are* brave enough, and I think you know that deep down." Madeline squeezed Lacy's hand again. "And don't ever forget that you've got me, cheering you on the whole way no matter what. From near or far, I'll always support you."

Lacy scooted her chair closer to Madeline's and leaned over to give her a hug. "Thank you," she whispered, fresh tears springing to her eyes.

These tears, though, were tears of gratitude and, she realized, of relief. She knew deep down that Madeline was right and, even deeper down, she already knew exactly what she wanted. Now it was just a matter of being brave enough to take that leap of faith.

CHAPTER TWENTY-FOUR

Colette stoked the fire in the stone hearth, prodding the glowing logs until they split and sent sparks flying up the chimney. The fire leaped and danced, filling the room with warmth and its cozy crackling sound. Satisfied that the fire would last a while longer, Colette added an extra log just in case and then settled back into her armchair. She and Emma were enjoying the early Saturday afternoon light and munching on Colette's freshly baked apple cinnamon muffins. It was their custom to enjoy a sweet treat most afternoons around this time, and it was yet another part of their predictable rhythms that brought Colette so much peace of mind.

"Delicious as always, my dear," Emma

commented, reaching for a second muffin. "I don't always have an appetite these days, but I *always* have room for one—or more—of your treats."

"Why do you think I always bake extra?" Colette teased, smiling at her surrogate mother. "I know these are your favorite."

"For good reason too. I dare you to find any person in the world who doesn't love your apple cinnamon muffins."

"Emma, you're too sweet," Colette said lightly, but Emma's praise never failed to lighten her heart. She picked up a muffin for herself and bit into it. The sweet softness of it melted in her mouth and, if she did say so herself, the muffins really were exceptional. She reached for her glass of milk and took a slow sip, simply enjoying the moment. Colette had nearly finished her muffin when her thoughts returned, as they had so many times since Emma had found the box, back to Lacy. "Emma," she said, breaking their companionable silence. "Do you think Lacy will come to understand her grandfather once she opens the box? Surely she'll have to see 'St. Nick' for who he was the way the rest of us did—the best and most generous of men."

Emma pursed her lips considering. "I don't know

what's in the box, but I'm sure it will clarify things. It's simply a matter of whether or not Lacy will open her heart to the truth."

"And do you think she will?"

"Dear, I'm sure of it. Lacy seems to have a good heart, and I think no one can fail to see the truth of Nicholas's true nature."

Colette sighed. "I wish I could be so sure of a good outcome. I just..." Colette reached out and took Emma's hand. "I just don't want you to be disappointed if things don't turn out the way you expect, that's all."

Emma patted Colette's hand reassuringly. "There's my sweet Colette, always looking out for my best interests. Don't worry, dear. Things have a way of working themselves out."

Colette leaned back in her chair, hoping Emma was right. Emma had such a soft heart, and she knew that although Emma hoped for the best, it would be a crushing blow to the older woman if Lacy continued to hate her grandfather and believe the worst in him. She reached for a second muffin, biting into it and chewing thoughtfully. No one could control the outcome of things—whatever would happen, would happen—but Colette instinctively wanted to protect

Emma from anything bad, even from disappointments such as this.

A knock at the door interrupted the moment and Colette rose to her feet. "Are we expecting anyone?"

"Not that I know of, dear."

Colette set her muffin on the plate beside her chair then, wiping her hands, she hurried to the front door and pulled it open. She felt her jaw drop open a little. To her utter surprise, Lacy stood on the front porch, her cheeks pink and her shoulders hunched against the cold. "Lacy! I thought you were supposed to be in St. Louis!"

"I couldn't wait and I came back early."

Colette stared at her, her mind trying to catch up. Lacy gave a nervous smile.

"Can I come in?"

Colette blinked, pulling herself together. "Of course, it's freezing out. Come in!"

Lacy hurried into the foyer, shivering. She carried two boxes in her arms, and Colette instantly recognized the wooden box Nicholas had left for her. Her heart began to thump painfully in her chest and she wondered what news Lacy would have for them and what it contained.

"I'm so sorry to just barge in like this," Lacy said, setting the boxes down and taking off her coat.

By then, Emma had gotten up from her chair and was walking toward them. "Hello, my dear! We weren't expecting you."

"I should have called ahead," Lacy said apologetically. "I know it's rude to show up unannounced, but..." She looked at the boxes resting by her feet, then up to Colette and Emma. "I haven't opened the box yet," she blurted. "I couldn't bear to do it alone in St. Louis, so I rushed back here. And knowing how special you were to Nicholas, Emma, I thought it only appropriate to open it with you here."

Emma reached out and touched Lacy's arm. "That was incredibly thoughtful of you."

Lacy flushed a little. "It's nothing. Besides, like I said, I couldn't bear to be alone, not after everything I've been learning over the past couple of days."

"What do you mean?" Colette asked.

Lacy gestured to the second box sitting atop Nicholas's wooden box. She opened it and showed them mounds of unopened letters. "My mother kept these from me. My father and grandfather tried to write to me over and over again for years, and I never knew."

"Oh, Lacy..." Colette reached out impulsively and gave her a hug. "Are you all right?"

Lacy clutched her back. "I'm not right now, but I

will be." She let go of Colette and wiped at a stray tear, giving a little laugh. "See? This is why I didn't want to do this alone. Discovering the letters alone was a lot to handle."

"We understand, dear," Emma said, patting Lacy's arm. "Come sit down with us and we'll take all the time you want to open the box."

"Thank you," Lacy said gratefully, gathering up the boxes.

Colette led the way to the sitting area, gesturing to the sofa, where Lacy settled herself. Her heart was already beating harder with the excitement of the moment, but also with some fear. It already seemed that Lacy had softened toward Nicholas, but now that left Colette hoping desperately that whatever was in the box would not hurt, but help, Lacy. She didn't know Lacy all that well, but she already held a liking for the woman.

"Well... I guess there's no point in putting it off," Lacy said nervously.

"Take all the time you need to," Emma said, her voice gentle. "The box isn't going anywhere."

"Thanks. I do think I'm ready now, though. It's all I've been thinking about since you gave it to me."

Lacy settled Nicholas's box on her lap and then

pulled a necklace out from beneath her shirt, revealing an intricate and delicate silver key. Lacy pulled in a deep breath, unclasping the necklace and looking at them for reassurance. Colette smiled at Lacy encouragingly and Lacy gave a somewhat wobbly smile back. With shaking fingers, Lacy finally managed to fit the key into the lock and turned it. Colette heard the audible click as the box unlocked and Lacy slowly lifted the lid.

Colette gasped aloud as she saw the stacks upon stacks of neatly bound money resting inside. Her eyes flew to Lacy's face, who had become pale as a ghost and sat, frozen, staring at the money with wide eyes and an open mouth.

"Mercy," Emma whispered beside her.

"What in the world," Lacy breathed. Her fingers still trembling violently, she reached in and picked up the letter that rested on top of the money and tore it open carefully, pulling a sheet of paper from within. "Colette, Emma, will one of you two read it for me? I don't think I can."

Colette reached out, knowing Emma's glasses were in another room. "I can do it," she said softly.

Lacy handed her the letter and Colette cleared her throat to read aloud.

"My dearest Lacy," she read. "How I wish I could be there with you to tell you all of this in person. I'm sure you must be filled with confusion and questions, but I'll do my best to answer them here. My sweet girl, I have watched your growth from afar for many years, and I am so incredibly proud of the woman you have become. The money you will find contained in this box is part of your inheritance, in addition to the mansion. Use it to make the mansion into something beautiful once again—I know you can do it. I wanted you to be the one to do it after watching your successes in the business world. I trust your business sense, my girl, and I know you will make a fine go of it. After all, it runs in the family. I leave the mansion and this money in your care, knowing it is in the best hands. I love you, my dear, more than you will ever know. Love, Your Grandpapa."

By the end of the letter, Colette was a little choked up and had a hard time getting Nicholas's tender words out. Lacy was silently weeping as she listened, reaching up now and again to wipe tears off her cheeks. Emma too, cried quietly, though her face was serene and peaceful. Quietly, Colette folded up the letter and returned it to Lacy, who clutched it to her chest for a moment.

"What an incredible gift," Lacy finally murmured. "I poured my life savings into the mansion, hoping to make it successful, and he lifted the burden I've been carrying, just like that." She shook her head, her eyes wide. "I still can't believe it."

"I knew he would do what he could to take care of you," Emma said, her voice loving. "That was simply always his way."

"I wish I could have known him. I wish I could have had time with him," Lacy said, her voice breaking. "I feel so cheated. I lost all those years to have a relationship with him and my father because my mother stole them from me." She dropped her head, her shoulders beginning to shake. "How could she do that to me? To all of us?"

Almost as one, Colette and Emma rose from their seats to sit on either side of Lacy and wrapped their arms around her, holding her as she sobbed quietly.

"Shh, shh," Emma soothed. "Let the pain out."

It took some time, but after a while, Lacy finally straightened, giving them a watery smile. "Thank you. Sometimes the pain just hits all over again, as fresh as when I first discovered the letters, and it's too much to stand."

"Your heart will begin to heal in time," Colette said, barely above a whisper. She knew this from painful experience.

"I hope so," Lacy responded. "I just wish I knew why she did it."

"You will never fully know," Emma said, "but I am certain that your mother loved you. If I were to guess based on what Nicholas told me, she was probably scared and doing what she thought was best to protect you. We all make mistakes when trying to care for the people we love, especially after we've been hurt ourselves. I know it's not my place, dear, but I hope you can forgive her. You deserve to find peace, and you won't find it if you harbor anger toward your mother."

Lacy nodded. "I know you're right, but I also know that it will take time."

"It will," Colette said, and reached out to squeeze Lacy's hand. She barely knew this woman, but she had already come to care for her as a friend.

"At least now I know the truth," Lacy said, reaching out to gently caress the letter Nicholas had left for her. "That's something."

"My dear," Emma said. "That is everything."

Lacy nodded, her eyes becoming clear. She

straightened her shoulders and took in a shuddering breath. "Well, you two, enough tears for now. After all, we have a party to plan in Nicholas's memory."

"To St. Nick," Colette said, with a soft smile.

The others echoed her. "To St. Nick."

CHAPTER TWENTY-FIVE

Lacy's heart felt like it was swelling as she watched a beautiful smile spread across Emma's wrinkled features. The old woman clapped her hands together, beaming with joy and she even laughed aloud. Colette reached out and squeezed Lacy's hand, her eyes speaking volumes about how grateful she was that Lacy had brought joy to Emma and, Lacy suspected, that she no longer believed the worst about Nicholas Spielman.

Although pain still lingered within, Lacy resolved then and there that she would not let the bitterness and anger at losing those years with her father and grandfather drag her down. It would be so easy to stop believing in the goodness of people, to close her heart off and hunker down emotionally to protect her heart from vulnerability and further loss, but she knew that was not the way. She had spent too many years steeling her soul against true connection with most people, angry at Harv and Nicholas for seeming to abandon her. No more, she resolved. From this moment onward she would try to focus on the positives, to allow herself to connect with others in meaningful ways.

Of course, a little voice in the back of her head spoke up, *your mother proves that people can hurt you in ways that can never be fixed. Maybe it* would *be better to keep on protecting your heart...*

Lacy shuddered in spite of herself and a spike of anger against her mother crashed over her.

No, she told herself fiercely. *No! I will not walk down that road again.*

The voice subsided after more of a struggle, and she knew that she would have to wade through that pain more than once before it was healed, but she put it aside for the present moment. As she had just said to Emma and Colette, they had a party to plan in Nicholas's honor.

"I poured so much of my savings into the house," she said aloud, running a finger over a stack of money in the box. "It wasn't enough to fully finish renovating the mansion, but it was a start. I'm just so grateful that now I can finish it and that it can be everything my grandfather always knew it could become."

"It will be glorious," Emma declared. "Personally, I'm beside myself with excitement at the prospect of seeing it, especially once it's all decorated for the Christmas party." She smiled at Lacy fondly. "Nicholas knew what he was doing when he left the mansion in your care."

Lacy flushed a little. "I have to admit that I didn't want it at first..."

"Well, why would you, believing what you did about Nicholas? I'm sure it must have felt like a burden."

"It did," Lacy agreed, remembering back to when the attorney had called her and informed her of her inheritance. "I spent so much time trying to figure out what to do with it, and I only cared about fixing it up so I could sell it and make a profit. Now, though... now I want to finish fixing it up as a way to honor my father and grandfather. To carry on the Spielman legacy."

"What a beautiful and noble mission, my dear. Nicholas would be so proud." Emma looked at Lacy thoughtfully, tapping a finger against her chin. "Did you ever consider, though, that perhaps *you* are the

Spielman legacy? You are the living embodiment of Nicholas and Harv's goodness."

Tears formed in the corners of Lacy's eyes and she felt a lump grow in her throat. Although she hardly felt worthy of such praise, the words touched her nonetheless. She resolved once again to live worthy of that legacy.

"Thank you," she whispered, her voice choked with emotion. Lacy wiped at her eyes and chuckled in spite of herself. "And here I said I was finished with tears!"

"You've had quite the day," Colette spoke up then, giving Lacy a warm look. "There's no shame in crying."

"No, there's not," Lacy agreed, "but I meant it when I said I've *got* to get busy working on that party." With that she rose, reaching out to give both women a hug. "I'll see both of you soon, okay? There's someone else I need to go see right now."

Colette gave Lacy a grin that seemed a touch too knowing and it took everything in Lacy not to blush to the roots of her hair. Emma stood as well, giving Lacy one last hug and admonishing her to visit again soon. Pulling on her coat and gathering the boxes, Lacy promised to do so and, soon enough, she was waving goodbye and hurrying down the front steps to head into town. Glancing over her shoulder, she saw Emma and Colette still waving from the window, and she gave them one last wave, her heart full.

It was a bit of a walk from Emma's cottage back into the main part of town, but Lacy didn't mind. She had more than enough to keep her mind occupied and the long walk allowed her to burn off some of the excess energy from the visit at Emma's house.

After all, discovering an enormous sum of money in the box left by her grandfather had sent all sorts of emotions running through her body, and it felt good to stride through the snowy streets and breathe in the icy air, even if it did burn her lungs a little.

Eventually, Winter Run Racing came into view and she headed toward it, more than ready to tell Derek about everything that had transpired in the short time since she'd said goodbye to him.

Derek must've caught sight of her from the large front window of his shop, because he pulled open the door before she even had a chance to knock. "Lacy?" His voice was full of surprise but also, she noticed, an excited joy that sent thrills through her. "I didn't think you'd be back yet!"

"I didn't think I would either, but here I am," she announced, smiling up at him.

"Come on in," he said, stepping out of the way. "I know a certain puppy that will be over the moon about her mama being back."

"So I'm her mama now?"

"You rescued her. Of course you're her new mama."

Lacy's heart sang at the thought and she was quick to follow him into the kennel room. Derek glanced over his shoulder at her as they walked, taking notice of the two boxes in her arms.

"Here, let me take those."

Lacy gratefully handed them off, and just in time too. As soon as she stepped foot into the kennel room, Missy barked excitedly and launched herself at Lacy, tail wagging like crazy. Lacy laughed, dropping to her knees and wrapping her arms around the dog, who licked her face over and over. Lacy wrinkled her nose at Missy's dog breath, but she didn't stop Missy from licking her, instead just enjoying the moment. She scratched behind Missy's ears and murmured sweet words to the puppy. When Missy had finally had her fill and wandered off to play with her toys, Lacy got back to her feet to find Derek watching her with a warm expression in his eyes.

"It really is good to have you in town again. I'm glad you're back early."

"Me too. I returned early because so much happened while I was gone. Can we sit down? I have so much to tell you I can barely think straight."

"Let's go to my office."

A couple of minutes later they were both settled in the old, mismatched chairs that sat across from Derek's paper-piled desk. Without preamble, Lacy launched into a description of all that had happened.

She told him about discovering the unopened letters that her mother had hidden from her, about the discovery that she had not been abandoned by her father and Nicholas, of bringing the key necklace and Nicholas's box to Emma's house, and about the piles of money and the letter he had left for her.

Derek leaned forward as he listened, his eyes widening at times. When she told him about the unopened letters, his expression held such sympathy for her pain that she could have cried on the spot, but she swallowed back the tears and kept going.

"It was such a surprise to see what my grandfather left me," Lacy finished.

Derek raked his fingers through his hair

thoughtfully. "You know, I'm not that surprised, myself. Nicholas was a planner, and it makes sense that he would leave you with the means to fix up the mansion."

"Well, it just goes to show that you were right about Nicholas all along." She sighed. "And I was so very, very wrong."

"Hey." He reached out and took Lacy's hand, threading his fingers through hers loosely. "You couldn't have known."

"I know now, though. It's only made me more determined than ever to make the Christmas party a success. Before, it was a way to showcase the mansion as a venue, but now I want to do it as a way to honor Nicholas. I want it to be amazing."

Before she could even ask, Derek smiled at her. "Can I help? I'm sure you still have a mountain of work to get the party ready."

Lacy was touched and she squeezed his hand gratefully. "A million times, yes! I can use all the help I can get. Thank you."

"Of course."

"Nicholas would be grateful to you for making sure his legacy lives on."

Derek reached out and cupped her cheek with his free hand and she relished the feel of it.

"That's probably true," he admitted, "but I'm not doing it for him. I'm doing it for you."

Lacy's heart thumped hard at his simple words and she suddenly found that she couldn't hold herself back any longer. Reaching for him, she leaned forward and pressed her lips to his, pouring all that was in her heart into a kiss.

* * *

Derek climbed out from beneath the bathroom sink and finished tightening the last bolt as Lacy watched. "Okay, go ahead and try turning the water on," he said.

Lacy turned the knob and, to her relief, water gushed from the faucet. "It works!"

"Huzzah," Derek joked.

Lacy grinned at him as he wiped his hands on a towel hanging from his belt loop. True to his word, Derek had spent the last several days helping her prepare for the party. They had worked through her massive to-do list, hanging wreaths and garlands, picking up load after load of red poinsettias, fixing the gas line for the enormous sitting room fireplace, and hanging what felt like a million twinkle lights. And then, of course, there had been the deep cleaning, talking to vendors, shoveling snow and, today, fixing the plumbing in both of the upstairs bathrooms to make sure they were usable for all of the guests.

To her surprise, far from feeling like work, the days had sped by as the two had completed the tasks side by side, joking and talking the entire time. And, she had found, all of the drive she usually poured into her investment work back in St. Louis had found a beautiful home in preparing for the party with Derek. She had always liked to keep busy and accomplish goals, and those needs had been beautifully fulfilled through restoring the mansion. It had come as something of a surprise to her, especially since she had been so loth to come to Snowy Pine Ridge in the first place. The mansion's restoration had felt like a burden, but through the process of working on it, she had discovered that she didn't need the bustle of the big city to feel like she had a sense of purpose.

A knock at the door pulled her from her thoughts. "That's probably Mr. Winston," Derek said. "I'll go talk to him."

Lacy nodded gratefully. Mr. Winston, an elderly man from town, had approached them to offer his services as a Santa for the children during the party.

He would take pictures and let the children tell him what they wanted for Christmas. And he wasn't the only one—various folks from town had stopped by, offering to serve as vendors for the food or as musicians to provide live music. She had been overwhelmed by such generosity as it had been the last thing she'd expected. Something like that, she had known all too well, would have been highly unlikely back home.

She left the bathroom, walking to the top of the stairs and waving down at Mr. Winston. She paused for a moment before descending the steps, watching Derek chat with the elderly man, her heart swelling. She realized with a jolt that she had spent so much of her life striving and working, all in search of something to fill the void within her. Now, as she watched Derek, her heart swelled and she had the sudden feeling that she just may have found exactly what she'd been looking for all along. The realization took her breath away, and she had to grab the banister for support. As she started walking down the steps, her mind swirled with one simple question: did she have the courage to hold onto what she had found?

CHAPTER TWENTY-SIX

Derek paused outside Lacy's door at the inn, taking a moment to straighten his tie and to pull in a deep breath. Tonight was the night of the Christmas party, the night that he and Lacy had worked countless hours to bring to fruition, and it was all coming to a head within the next two hours. He hoped that everything would run smoothly for Lacy—he knew how much this party meant to her, especially now that she understood the truth about who Nicholas Spielman really had been. Taking in one last deep breath, he knocked on her door.

A moment later, Lacy answered and, as she did so, absolutely stole the breath from his body. She wore an emerald green velvet gown that brought out the startling green of her eyes, her hair loosely curled over her shoulders. She was, in a word, stunning. It was all he could do to keep his jaw from dropping open at the sight of her.

"Do I look that bad?" she teased, pulling on her coat.

"N-no, it's not—"

He broke off in some confusion, inwardly screaming at himself to gain control of his stammering tongue. Every part of him ached to beg her to stay in Snowy Pine Ridge, to ask her not to leave again, but he knew that was selfish.

Besides, tonight was about Lacy and honoring Nicholas's legacy, not about his wishes. He refused to make it about himself, so he simply took a breath and said, "Wow. You look gorgeous."

Lacy's cheeks flushed a little at his praise, but in usual Lacy manner, she brushed off her embarrassment with a joke.

"Stoppp," she said in an exaggerated drawl. "You're just saying that because it's true."

Derek laughed aloud at that and stepped forward to pull her into his arms. "You're a rogue and a scoundrel, Lacy Preston," he murmured, lowering his head to drop a kiss to her lips.

"Guilty as charged," she agreed cheerfully, before reaching up to bend his neck back down so she could kiss him one last time. "Come on, we've got a party to host."

"At your service, madam." Derek gave her a playful bow, extending his arm for her to take.

With a soft chuckle, Lacy tucked her hand into the crook of his elbow and they walked down the steps to the foyer and then out into the cold night. He opened the door of the truck and lifted her into it, tucking her dress carefully around her feet before hurrying around to the driver's side and starting the engine. They listened to Christmas music as they drove, holding hands and enjoying the quiet of the drive. Nicholas's mansion appeared in the distance, glittering and twinkling with all of the twinkle lights lit up. Derek sucked in a breath at the sight of it.

"This is amazing. It looks like a dream, and we haven't even gotten inside yet."

Lacy was smiling, her eyes reflecting the glow of the lights as he parked the truck. "It's everything I hoped it would be. And more."

"I'm glad," he said simply.

Once inside the mansion, they walked through each room, checking that everything was in place and ready for the guests who were set to arrive within the next half hour. Sarah was busy setting up her booth full of delicious-looking baked goods, the live band was tuning up their instruments in the ballroom, and the girl running coat-check was getting set up.

In the ballroom, small round tables covered in green and red checked tablecloths lined the perimeter of the dance floor. All of the rooms were lavishly decorated and the heady scent of fresh pine permeated the mansion.

Derek reached out and took Lacy's hand as they returned to the front foyer. "Are you ready?"

"I think so," she replied, absentmindedly running her thumb across the side of his hand, sending electric sparks up the length of his arm. "It's beautiful to think of seeing this place filled with laughter and love the way my grandfather—St. Nick —loved it to be."

"I like to think he's watching over us tonight and that he's pleased."

"I hope so. I want to learn more about him from Emma as time goes on. As much as I can. Maybe it will help to make up for all the time I lost with him."

Derek pulled in a breath, wondering if she realized what she had just said. If she was hoping to learn more from Emma as time went on, maybe that meant she wasn't planning to stay away from Snowy Pine Ridge for good...

Don't get your hopes up, he reminded himself sternly, *and don't bring it up right now. Guests are about to arrive, and Lacy doesn't need to be distracted by your foolish hopes and dreams.*

As if on cue, the first group of guests arrived, walking up the front steps and spilling into the foyer. Lacy stepped forward to greet them, smiling graciously and introducing herself as the guests began handing their coats and wraps to the coat-check girl. Derek, seeing that Lacy was in her element and didn't appear to need any help, began to mingle with the guests as well. He knew most of the townspeople, and he was soon caught up in catching up with old friends and directing guests to the ballroom and to the vendors' booths.

A jovial and festive atmosphere enveloped everyone at the party as more and more guests arrived, dressed up in their best Christmas gowns and suits. Derek was just about to go check on the guests in the ballroom when Colette and Emma arrived. He called to Lacy and hurried over to greet them, helping Emma to take off her coat. She was lavishly dressed in a maroon gown with sparkles and rhinestones, her fluffy white hair swept up into a French twist. Her eyes sparkled with unshed tears of happiness as she took in the beautifully restored and decorated mansion. She raised a trembling hand and pressed it against her lips.

"Oh," she breathed. "Oh, Nicholas would have been so proud." She turned to Lacy, taking Derek's arm and leaning against him. "I wish he could see how beautifully you've arranged everything."

Derek patted her hand. "I'm certain he is seeing it." He glanced over at Lacy, who he realized was standing still and silent, and saw that a conflict was raging in her eyes.

"Thank you so much," Lacy finally choked out. "I have to see to something, please excuse me."

Without another word of explanation, Lacy turned on her heel and plunged into the crowd, disappearing from sight. Derek ached for her, knowing that something was deeply wrong and wanting very much to talk to her about it, but Emma still hung on his arm. Colette, seeing his distress, stepped up and gently disengaged Emma, telling her they should go and try some of Sarah's baked goods. Derek sent her a thankful glance and then scanned the party—he needed to go find Lacy.

* * *

Lacy slipped through the guests in the ballroom and stepped out onto the beautifully lit wrap-around porch. Wrapping her arms around herself for warmth, she relished a break from the happy noise inside and gulped in the fresh, icy air. Although she was pleased that the party was going so well, she was suddenly overcome with a storm of emotion. Seeing Emma enjoying the party had struck a raw chord inside of herself. It wasn't that she was jealous, exactly, but she had realized only moments before that Emma knew her grandfather so deeply— something she herself would never experience.

Tears prickled at the corners of her eyes and a lump grew in her throat. How she wished that she could turn back the years and get to spend them with her father and grandfather.

Stop wishing for something you can never have, she scolded herself.

In that moment, she realized more than ever that she had misunderstood Harv and Nicholas her whole life. Nicholas had never stopped believing in her, as was all too evident from the legacy he had left for her.

But as for herself? She had stopped believing in them as soon as her mother had told her they had been abandoned. She had built her entire life, her education, her career, around distancing herself from Harv and Nicholas. It made her wonder what the point was of the life she had built in St. Louis.

Had it been built out of spite? She cringed as she knew that the answer was a resounding *yes*.

Hearing footsteps coming up behind her, Lacy straightened and tried to look carefree and unaffected. She turned around, ready to greet another guest and then sighed with relief as she saw Derek walking toward her, his forehead creased with concern.

"Are you all right?"

Lacy bit her lip. "I don't know. I think so?"

Derek reached for her, pulling her into his arms and nestling her close to him. "If you're worried about the party, it's going splendidly. Everyone's talking about what an amazing job you've done."

"I'm glad. I hoped it would be a success," she replied.

"Now that we've all seen what you can do, I think I speak for everyone when I say you better come back to visit often. Snowy Pine Ridge won't be the same without you."

Lacy hesitated, the idea she'd been mulling over for days resting on the edge of her tongue. Gathering her courage, she pulled back enough to search his eyes. "What would you think if I stayed in Snowy Pine Ridge for good?"

Derek's jaw dropped, his eyes wide with shock. "What in the world brought this on? I thought you couldn't wait to get back to St. Louis?"

"I've been thinking about it for a while now," she admitted, then sighed. "I've been realizing that the life and business I built back in St. Louis was all about trying to forget about my father and grandfather. Trying to distance my name from theirs as much as I could. Now... well, now that doesn't seem so important anymore. I think it really hit home for me tonight that I did all that to give myself a sense of worth because I felt like I lost all of that when my grandfather and father left."

"Oh, Lacy..." Derek pulled her closer, resting his cheek on her hair. "I wish I could go back in time and spare you all of that pain."

Lacy clung to him. "Me too," she murmured. "But I'm okay now, I promise. Or, at least, I'm getting there." She pulled back again so that she could look at him. "Now that these things have been clarified for me, I've been thinking that maybe Snowy Pine Ridge could use a seasoned financial and loans consultant like myself on a semi-permanent basis."

Derek gave her a crooked grin and leaned down to kiss her. "The more permanent the better."

Lacy laughed. "This town has sort of stolen my heart, you know, so that just might happen."

"Just the town?" Derek teased, but there was a look in his eyes that made Lacy's heart race.

Before she could answer, Derek took her hand and tugged it gently, pulling her back through the ballroom, weaving through the couples dancing. Soon he was helping her shrug into her coat and pulling his on as well.

"What are you doing?" Lacy asked, laughing.

Derek pinned her with a look. "I want to get away with you."

"Get away...?" Lacy asked as Derek pulled her out onto the front porch and down the front steps.

Instead of answering, Derek whistled and, a moment later, she heard the jingling of bells as Derek's dogsled team trotted up. Lacy gaped, amazed to see the team waiting obediently and turned to stare at Derek.

"You want to leave on a dogsled? The moonlit dogsled rides aren't supposed to start for another hour!"

"The advantage of being in charge of the dogsled

rides," Derek pointed out, "is that I can change the schedule whenever I want."

With that, Derek scooped Lacy up and set her on the sled, climbing up behind her as her laughter rang out through the night. Wrapping his arms around her, Derek whistled and called out a command to his team and they plunged forward, taking off into the night. As they flew over the snow, Lacy nestled into Derek's arms, relishing the wind whipping through her hair. Certainty spread through her as Derek guided the team through the festively-lit town, and she knew deep in her bones that she was exactly where she belonged, especially with Derek by her side.

"Having fun?" Derek asked in her ear.

Lacy twisted a little so she could look up at him, nodding.

"This might just be the best night of my life," she told him truthfully, hope and love bursting in her chest. "And I can't wait to see what comes next."

* * *

The series continues in *Sweet Christmas Wish*!

ALSO BY FIONA BAKER

The Marigold Island Series

The Beachside Inn

Beachside Beginnings

Beachside Promises

Beachside Secrets

Beachside Memories

Beachside Weddings

Beachside Holidays

Beachside Treasures

The Sea Breeze Cove Series

The House by the Shore

A Season of Second Chances

A Secret in the Tides

The Promise of Forever

A Haven in the Cove

The Blessing of Tomorrow

A Memory of Moonlight

The Snowy Pine Ridge Series

The Christmas Lodge

Sweet Christmas Wish

Second Chance Christmas

Christmas at the Guest House

For a full list of my books and series, visit my website at www.fionabakerauthor.com!

ABOUT THE AUTHOR

Fiona writes sweet, feel-good contemporary women's fiction and family sagas with a bit of romance.

She hopes her characters will start to feel like old friends as you follow them on their journeys of love, family, friendship, and new beginnings. Her heartwarming storylines and charming small-town beach settings are a particular favorite of readers.

When she's not writing, she loves eating good meals with friends, trying out new recipes, and finding the perfect glass of wine to pair them with. She lives on the East Coast with her husband and their two trouble-making dogs.

Follow her on her website, Facebook, or Bookbub.

Sign up to receive her newsletter, where you'll get free books, exclusive bonus content, and info on her new releases and sales!